A Guide to the
Birds of East Africa

A NOVEL

NICHOLAS DRAYSON

VIKING
an imprint of
PENGUIN BOOKS

VIKING

Published by the Penguin Group
Penguin Books Ltd, 80 Strand, London WC2R ORL, England
Penguin Group (USA) Inc., 375 Hudson Street, New York, New York 10014, USA
Penguin Group (Canada), 90 Eglinton Avenue East, Suite 700, Toronto, Ontario, Canada M4P 2Y3
(a division of Pearson Penguin Canada Inc.)
Penguin Ireland, 25 St Stephen's Green, Dublin 2, Ireland (a division of Penguin Books Ltd)
Penguin Group (Australia), 250 Camberwell Road,
Camberwell, Victoria 3124, Australia (a division of Pearson Australia Group Pty Ltd)
Penguin Books India Pvt Ltd, 11 Community Centre,
Panchsheel Park, New Delhi – 110 017, India
Penguin Group (NZ), 67 Apollo Drive, Rosedale, North Shore 0632, New Zealand
(a division of Pearson New Zealand Ltd)
Penguin Books (South Africa) (Pty) Ltd, 24 Sturdee Avenue,
Rosebank, Johannesburg 2196, South Africa

Penguin Books Ltd, Registered Offices: 80 Strand, London WC2R ORL, England

www.penguin.com

First published 2008
1

Typeset in Monotype Dante by Palimpsest Book Production Limited,
Grangemouth, Stirlingshire
Printed in Great Britain by Clays Ltd, St Ives plc

A CIP catalogue record for this book is available from the British Library

Hardback ISBN: 978-0-670-917570
Trade paperback ISBN: 978-0-670-91758-7

www.greenpenguin.co.uk

For Bernadette

Black Kite

I

'Ah yes,' said Rose Mbikwa, looking up at the large dark bird with elegant tail soaring high above the car park of the Nairobi Museum, 'a black kite. Which is, of course, not black but brown.'

Mr Malik smiled. How many times had he heard Rose Mbikwa say those words? Almost as many times as he had been on the Tuesday morning bird walk.

You never know exactly how many kinds of birds you will see on the Tuesday morning bird walk of the East African Ornithological Society but you can be sure to see a kite. Expert scavengers, they thrive on the detritus of human society in and around Nairobi. At his first school sports day (how many years ago was that now – could it really be fifty?) Mr Malik remembered little of the sprinting and javelin throwing and fathers' sack race but he would never forget the kite which swooped down from nowhere to snatch a devilled chicken leg from his very hand. He could still recall the brush of feathers against his face and that single moment when as the bird's talons closed around the prize its yellow eye looked into his. Of course it wasn't quite accurate to say that he had no memories of the javelin throwing. Few would forget the incident with the Governor General's wife's corgi.

There was already a good turnout. Seated along the low wall in front of the museum a gaggle of Young Ornithologists (YOs), mostly students training to be tourist guides, chattered and preened. The Old Hands were also out in force. Joan Baker and Hilary Fotherington-Thomas were leaning against a car talking to a couple of pink-faced men, one bearded, whose pocket-infested khaki clothing instantly identified them as tourists and their accents as Australian. Standing furtively to one side were Patsy King and Jonathan Evans. They had been carrying on their Tuesday morning affair for almost two years now and though Mr Malik had never had an affair, he supposed that a certain furtiveness was necessary to achieve full satisfaction in these things. The two were an unlikely match. Imagine a giraffe, towering above the wide savannah. Now imagine a warthog. But Mr Malik was used to seeing the lanky figure of Patsy King striding along road or track, her 10 x 50 binoculars enveloped in one large hand, with Jonathan Evans trotting along beside her. To Mr Malik they seemed, like members of his own family, no longer remarkable.

Keeping himself to himself as usual was Thomas Nyambe. He was standing with his back to the crowd, looking up towards the sky, entranced. Mr Nyambe loved birds, and had been coming to the bird walks even longer than Mr Malik. Tuesday was his rostered morning off from his job as government driver. A driver in Kenya is seldom paid enough to afford a car of his own, so as usual Mr Nyambe had walked to the museum from his home in Factory Road, just behind the railway station. As usual Mr Malik would offer him a lift to wherever they were going that day.

A bang and a rattle and a loud curse through an open window announced the arrival of Tom Turnbull driving over the speed bump in his yellow Morris Minor (the speed bump had been there

2

over a year now but still it took him by surprise). He opened the door of the car, got out, and slammed it. He cursed, opened the door, and slammed it again. The distant town hall clock struck nine.

'Good morning and welcome,' said Rose.

All conversation ceased, all heads turned.

'I see a few new faces here – and many old ones – but I welcome all of you to the Tuesday morning bird walk. My name is Rose Mbikwa.'

Mr Malik had got used to it by now, the transformation of Rose's normal low contralto speaking voice into her public voice of distance-shrinking volume and clarity. Rose looked around the group, nodding here and smiling there, then conferred again with the young woman who had earlier pointed out the kite.

'And to those of you who don't know her, may I introduce Jennifer Halutu. Just to remind you, I will be away next week and Jennifer will be leading the walk. Last week, you may remember, we thought we might try the MEATI but we didn't have enough cars. Do we have enough this week?' She looked around the car park. 'I think we might. Who can give lifts?'

Hands were raised, calculations made.

'Good, that's fine,' said Rose. 'Then the MEATI it is. You all know the way?'

It was left to Joan Baker and Hilary Fotherington-Thomas to explain to the mystified newcomers that the Modern East African Tourist Inn was a popular restaurant on the southern outskirts of town.

Thomas Nyambe had already slipped into the front seat of Mr Malik's old green Mercedes 450 SEL. The back seats were still empty. Perhaps, thought Mr Malik, the two tourists would like to come with him? He was about to offer a lift when another Mercedes, a shiny red SL 350, bounced in over the speed bump and swung into the car park. A tinted window opened, a sunglassed face leaned out over gold-braceleted arm.

3

'Hi, Rose – not too late?' The man leapt out of the car. 'Hey, David, George, there you are. Your chariot awaits.'

The tourists, who Mr Malik now surmised were called David and George, walked over to the red Mercedes to be greeted with handshakes, smiles and shoulder clasps.

'These guys are staying at the Hilton too, Rose, so I said they should come along. OK with you?'

After the three of them had gained Rose's approval and paid their visitor's subscription the two guests were shown into the passenger seats while the driver jumped back behind the wheel, started the engine and pulled out on to the drive, yelling out through the window just before it closed.

'See you there, everyone.'

Who on earth was that? Brown skin, white hair, expensive clothing, and some kind of American accent; yet he looked slightly familiar. Mr Malik had little time to ponder this question, nor how this man seemed to know Rose Mbikwa, before several young black Africans piled into the back of his old Mercedes. The rest of the YOs slipped and squeezed into Rose's 504, Tom's Morris Minor and the assortment of Land Rovers, Toyotas and other vehicles that other Old Hands had brought along. Engines were started, handbrakes released. As he drove gently over the speed bump and eased his tightly packed load out into the morning traffic, Mr Malik was wearing a worried expression.

That man. No, it couldn't be. Not after all this time.

Pale
Chanting
Goshawk

2

Before we find out more about the mysterious stranger I should tell you a little more about Mr Malik, and about Rose.

Almost every Tuesday for sixteen years, at half past eight rain or shine, Rose Mbikwa has pulled up outside the museum in her Peugeot 504 station wagon. She bought the car in 1980, the year after a 504 won the International East African Safari Rally for the third time running. In those days it was just as easy to drive her son to school as have him hanging round for the school bus (Rose liked driving and refused to have a driver, even later when things got bad). Besides you saw more birds early in the morning if you were out and about, and she had always liked birds. But when Rose's husband was first arrested she thought it best that her son was out of the way. He was packed off to boarding school close to where her parents still lived in the house where she had grown up, just opposite the thirteenth hole of the Merchants' golf course in Morningside, Edinburgh.

Did you see Rose as a black woman? No, she is a white woman. Rose Macdonald as she then was, red of hair and fair of skin, had gone to Kenya in 1970. It was to be a holiday, an Abercrombie & Kent gift from her parents for passing her final law examinations. A glorious future lay ahead of her. Had she not already secured a fine position with Harrington, Harrington, McBrace and Harcourt, Advocates and Solicitors? In time, said her mother, she might even marry one of the partners. By the time Rose was due to go home to be awarded her degree and start work at the lawyers' office just off Princes Street she'd had second thoughts about a lifetime of torts and conveyancing and fallen in love with Kenya – and with one particular inhabitant thereof. Despite simultaneous storms in Morningside and the Muthaiga Club she and Joshua Mbikwa, who had just finished his doctorate in physical anthropology but had a passion for politics, were married at the Holy Family cathedral in Nairobi on 16th July 1971. Joshua was elected to parliament the following October and their son Angus was born the following month. Joshua Mbikwa was re-elected in 1977, arrested for the first time in 1985 (just a warning, so they said) and in 1988 became Deputy Leader of the Opposition. In December of the following year he was again arrested, charged with sedition, convicted and imprisoned. While Rose spent her days and nights campaigning for her husband's release and writing letters to anyone important she knew or could think of, she also began to study the plants and animals around her. In both tasks she succeeded. Her campaign created such pressure within Kenya and without that Joshua Mbikwa was released, exonerated and reinstated in parliament, while Rose herself found that she had become just as entranced by African bulbuls and weaver birds as she had ever been by the blackbirds and thrushes of Scotland.

When Joshua was killed five months later in that unfortunate and mysterious accident with the light plane, the President himself assured her that he was just as distraught as he knew she must be and insisted she call him personally if there was anything he could do to make her return to the UK as painless as possible. Rose Mbikwa, who now loved Kenya as fiercely as her husband had loved it and knew more about the plants and animals and politicians of the country than most people who had been born there, thanked him for his kindness. The next day she went along to the office of the East African Ornithological Society at Nairobi Museum and joined up, paying three years' subscription in advance.

When the time came for Rose to renew her subscription Angus had moved on from his beloved boarding school in Edinburgh to study international relations (both of them were amused by the idea) at the University of St Andrews, but she was still living in the same house in Serengeti Gardens, Hatton Rise, Nairobi. And she had developed a plan. Just because her beloved husband was dead did not mean his convictions and his work for a better Kenya should die with him. It was becoming clear that Kenya, buffeted by the winds of global change while shackled by the chains of internal corruption, needed help. Rose could see one bright light on the horizon and it did not involve the law. It was tourism. What did people come to Kenya to see? The wildlife. Who was training local tourist guides to show them the wild-life? No one. Surely, thought Rose, this was something the Nairobi Museum could get involved in. With its team of curators, and its collections and displays on plants and animals, land and land-scape and people past and present, the museum would be an ideal focus for a comprehensive tourist guide training programme.

Rose worked behind the scenes, advocating, soliciting, persuading, planning. There was no money for such a scheme, of course, but now that her son had finished his schooling she was happy to contribute a part of what remained of her own small inheritance to get it up and going. Her husband, she was sure, would have done the same. The measure of her success was that when the Minister of Tourism and the Minister of Education called a joint news conference to announce the training programme which she had designed, each seemed to think that he alone was responsible for the whole idea.

Rose accepted the position of programme coordinator and

leader, a position she still holds. Chances are that if you go on safari in Kenya today your guide will have trained in the programme – listen for the trace of a Scottish accent. But Rose still loves her birds, and as Honorary Secretary (Expeditions) of the EAOS still takes each Tuesday morning off from her main job to lead the bird walk as she has been doing almost every week for the last sixteen years. Though most of her red hairs are now white her enthusiasm is undimmed, her knowledge is unmatched, and her car is now as old and battered as any other Peugeot 504 anywhere else in Africa.

Mr Malik, as you already have guessed, is neither black nor white. He is a brown man, sixty-one years old, short, round and balding. Most men go bald. Be in possession of one X and one Y chromosome, live long enough, and at some stage you will find your hair thinning, receding or just plain disappearing, and the fact that follicles which depart the scalp seem to appear reinvigorated in nostrils and ears is usually of small consolation. So men are sooner or later faced with a choice – live with it, or fight back.

Mr Malik had just turned thirty-two when, on a visit to his barber at the shop in Nkomo Avenue where he had been going for his regular fortnightly cut and style since well before Nkomo Avenue had changed its name from King George Street, he was informed that sir was 'going a little thin on top'. To a man proud of his sleek locks, this was less than welcome news. His barber went on to suggest that perhaps it might be time for a new style.

It has to be said that on aesthetic grounds alone this suggestion had some merit. The Brylcreemed quiff that a daring young Mr Malik had brought back from London in the early 1960s may have caused a satisfying intake of breath from the short-back-and-sides Nairobi of the time, but this was 1976. If an impression of a serious man of business was what you wished to create – which by now Mr Malik did – a Brylcreemed quiff and four-inch side-burns were probably not the best way to go about creating it.

'Perhaps something a little more formal, sir. Formal, but not old-fashioned.'

Sir, having just had his hair washed and being now in the process of having his scalp massaged, was feeling both blissful and benign.

'Did you have anything in mind?'

From a shelf above the basin the barber whipped down one of several loose-leaf folders.

'I'm thinking tapered at the sides but straight Boston at the back,' he said, flicking through the pages. 'Sideburns if sir insists but no more than three-quarters of an inch. Something like this, perhaps?'

He thrust the book in front of his seated and robed customer. The page showed the Hollywood actor Rock Hudson in a publicity still for a recent film. It appeared, from the bandana round the actor's neck and the check shirt, to be a western. Mr Malik had long had a soft spot for Rock Hudson – especially in those films with Doris Day (if he had a soft spot for Rock Hudson he went all squishy when he thought about the divine Miss Day). He looked hard at the picture. Rock Hudson was also wearing a fairly substantial moustache and unless he had a very small head his sideburns were well over three-quarters of an inch long but the overall effect looked modern enough. If he half closed his eyes Mr Malik even thought he could see the hint of a quiff.

With the aid of combs and mirrors the barber demonstrated another advantage of this new style. If sir's hair was parted just a little further over to the right, the thin patch would be undetectable. Mr Malik agreed, leaving the shop with a new hairstyle and a confident spring in his step, and the barber with a more than generous tip. And call it coincidence if you will but just a few weeks later Mrs Malik announced that seven years and one month after their one and only son had been born, she was again pregnant.

As his little daughter Petula grew taller and fatter, Mr Malik's thin patch grew thinner and wider. At first this was not a problem. Mr Malik discovered that all he had to do was move his parting just a fraction further towards the right so that more hair was available above the parting to cover the thin bit. When it got thinner still he found that a little Brylcreem (of which a large jar remained at the back of the bathroom cupboard from his quiff days) helped the hair to stay in place. Gradually, almost imperceptibly, the parting got lower, the Brylcreem thicker. Now there was no doubt about it. What had begun thirty years ago as a straight Rock Hudson had developed into a classic comb-over.

The now grown-up (and slimmed-down) Petula might tease him about it, the abominably hairy Patel might make sly references at the club to certain British footballers known for their adherence to the style. His barber might suggest that perhaps it was time sir might like to think about a toupee (his wife was by now sadly deceased and so silent on the matter). But one major change of hairstyle in life was enough in any man. Wigs were out, and he would not go from a covered scalp to a bare one no matter how long it now took him every morning to arrange each hair, and no matter how unconvincing the effect might be. But it is a little-appreciated truth that a bad hairstyle neither reflects nor affects the heart within. Passions burn as fiercely in Mr Malik's breast as in those of other men.

For the last three years Mr Malik – brown, short, round and balding though he may be – has been passionately in love with Rose Mbikwa.

3

When his wife Aruna had died from cancer eight years earlier, Mr Malik's response, like that of many men in similar situations, had been to throw himself into his work. He had loved his wife. Not at first, not when introduced to the shy girl that their families had chosen to be his wife. She was rather on the tall side, he thought, and only a little bit pretty. But soon he came to know this deep and quiet girl, and as she grew into a woman he was impressed by her strengths, which were many, and endeared by her weaknesses, which were few. And beauty seemed to grow within her. It sometimes shone so bright he could hardly look at her. Her death caused a pain that stabbed into his soul, a pain that only ceaseless work could ease. When he suffered his first heart attack – at exactly the same age as his own father had suffered one and died from it – his daughter Petula insisted he see a specialist.

'And I'm talking Harley Street here, Daddy, not Limuru Road.'

Mr Malik was not a poor man. The Jolly Man Manufacturing Company had been started by his father in 1932. This was the time when everyone seemed to smoke. Smoking was cool. Men smoked pipes, rich men smoked cigars, and women from maids to marchionesses smoked cigarettes. Everybody in films smoked – even Rock Hudson (though not, perhaps, Doris Day). In the Kenya of those far-off days imported cigarettes and cigars were sometimes hard to come by. Why not, thought Mr Malik senior, buy some tobacco, find some equipment and start making them himself? The Jolly Man Manufacturing Company, with its trademark picture of a smiling dark-skinned man in top hat and tailcoat puffing on a fat cigar, was an immediate success.

Then came the Second World War. German U-boats patrolled the Atlantic and supplies to Britain of tobacco from America and the West Indies dried up. Kenya was part of the British Empire and Kenyan tobacco was requisitioned for British manufacturers. Output from the Jolly Man Manufacturing Company slowed to a trickle. As soon as the war ended the big international companies came in with their Navy Cut and Pall Malls and Lucky Strikes. The Jolly Man Manufacturing Company, with its old and inefficient machinery, could not compete. Things looked bad. But during the war Jolly Man cigars had become a great favourite of Mikael Oncratoff, the Russian consul (everyone knew he was really a spy, but he gave such wonderful parties). When the war ended he began sending boxes of the Kenyan cigars home to his family and friends in Eastern Europe. Being superior to the local product and cheaper than Cuban cigars, they were in high demand. So great became their popularity behind the newly forged Iron Curtain that he approached Mr Malik senior – perhaps he needed an export agent? By 1960 Mikael Oncratoff had a fine house beside Lake Como, while discerning comrades from Gdansk and Stalingrad to Sofia and the Black Sea demanded Jolly Man cigars. And Mr Malik's father employed three hundred people in his factory in Nairobi making them. In 1964 he had his heart attack.

By this time Mr Malik had left school and been sent to study at the London School of Economics. Though economics did not interest him in the least (the LSE had been his father's idea), he loved London. He found digs in Clerkenwell and under those grey northern skies he blossomed as he never had in equatorial sunshine. He loved the pubs, the streets, the women, the freedom, the whole student life. He began writing the occasional piece on student politics for the University of London student newspaper (at that time still *The Ferret*), and the talent for journalism that he discovered within thrilled him so much he would often walk home from lectures along Fleet Street just for a glimpse into a real newspaper office and a fragrant whiff of printer's ink. Perhaps, when he finished his degree, he would become a journalist. Then the telegram came. Like the dutiful eldest son he was he gave all this up, came home for the funeral and took up his position as reluctant proprietor and Managing Director of the Jolly Man Manufacturing Company.

In the sense that he had always looked after his staff well and the business made money, Mr Malik was a good businessman. In the sense that he couldn't stop worrying about the business all day and all night and all times in between, he was a bad one. When he wasn't worrying about his business he was worrying about his daughter Petula. Petula had also been educated overseas and had returned home in 2001 with an MBA from NYC but without a husband. She was now twenty-nine, still unmarried and living at home. It was enough to worry any father – and if only she wouldn't cut her hair so short and would wear a nice sari occasionally instead of those baggy jeans all the time. 'Not jeans, Daddy – denims,' she said, but they still looked like jeans to him. He had to admit, though, that Petula had become a great help in running the business.

'I've made an appointment for you in London with Sir Horatio Redmond,' she told him. 'Don't worry, Daddy, I'll keep things ticking over while you're away.'

What Sir Horatio, staring over rooftops under a grey Marylebone sky to the bare trees of Regent's Park, said to his new patient was this:

'You need a hobby. Something to take your mind off work – it's stress that does it, you see.'

The eminent cardiologist savoured the word. Up until only last year he would have said 'overdoing it' and he still wasn't sure whether that phrase was really a bit more Harley Street, but everyone seemed to use 'stress' these days and it was good practice to keep up with modern developments. Patients expected it.

A large grey bird flapped slowly through the gloom towards the park. Bloody heron – what was that doing here? Trout-murdering vermin. The doctor turned from the window with a frown. Were there, he wondered as he watched his dark-skinned patient do up the top button of his shirt and reach for his bow tie, trout in India – no, Africa, wasn't it? He still remembered snatches from the lectures in tropical diseases at Barts. Mosquitoes and malaria, blackfly and river fever, tsetse and sleeping sickness – yes, they had plenty of flies in Africa. But did they have duns and drones, skippers and sedges? Did highland burns dash down from Afric hills and slow chalk streams meander through gentle meadows wherever it was that this chap came from?

'I fish myself,' he said, assuming once more the demeanour which his rank and rent allowed him. 'But for you, I think, birds.'

Mr Malik, whose residence in the London of the 1960s had coincided with the brief and wonderful emergence of the 'dolly bird', was puzzled. Was this man suggesting that he find another wife? Or perhaps revitalize himself through the prophylactic of prostitution?

'Sparrows, now,' said Sir Horatio. 'Why, a chap I know used to sit for hours and watch sparrows. Very soothing, so he told me. Sparrows flying, sparrows hopping, sparrows feeding, sparrows nesting. You have sparrows in, er . . . ?'

'Kenya.'

'Quite.'

'Yes.'

'Good. Well, that's it, then. Oh, and take one of these green pills, three times a day before meals.'

Mr Malik breathed an inward sigh of relief. Ornithology would be much easier – so much less stressful – than women. On the way home to Nairobi he picked up a pair of Bausch & Lomb 8 x 50 binoculars duty-free at Heathrow. He was surprised to find that during his absence the business seemed to have carried on very well without him.

The very next Tuesday he began his acquaintance with the birds of East Africa, and with Rose Mbikwa.

Olive Thrush

4

By the time Mr Malik got to the MEATI most of the others had arrived and were surveying the surrounding bush for birds. The man with the sunglasses and gold bangles (and, Mr Malik now noticed, a gold chain round his neck) was standing next to the tourists. He was pointing to a tree but broke off his conversation when Mr Malik got out of his car.

'Hey, Malik, is that you?'

And it all came flooding back. Harry Khan.

As an invalid in long remission may almost forget his illness until it returns, so it was with Mr Malik and Harry Khan. Mr Malik had been eleven when first struck down. He was a new boy at Eastlands High School, a boarder. So was Harry Khan. They were put into the same class and it was generally expected that the two new students ('new bugs' they were called in a faint echo of the language of an English public school) would get along. They didn't. Mr Malik, or just plain Malik as he was now known to both teachers and pupils, was a shy and studious boy. Harry Khan was – well, how shall I put it? He was loud, though

16

not in an obnoxious way. He was cheeky, though not in an impolite way. He was humorous, though not in an offensive way. He was clever without appearing to try hard; he made friends easily and had a quickness of foot in rugby and undoubted skill with a cricket ball and bat. It was Harry Khan who smuggled in the electric toaster to the dormitory, it was he who kept the radio under his mattress for tuning into the BBC World Service for *The Goon Show* on Saturday nights, it was he who introduced the younger (and some of the older) pupils to other nocturnal delights. He could even dance rock and roll. All of which made him popular among the boys, but for the next seven years he was the bane of Mr Malik's life. For Harry Khan was a tease, a card, a joker – and for every joker there has to be a jokee. It had started on the very first morning.

Now it has to be said that Harry Khan, were you to ask him even today, would still maintain that it wasn't his fault. It seems that what happened was this. The two new boys, having survived their first night in Middle Dorm, were in the splasher washing faces and cleaning teeth before brekker. Mr Malik's mother had packed her son's trunk with everything on the list she had been sent by Matron including a fine new plastic BOAC zip-up sponge bag – also containing everything that the list said should be there. Though sponges were notable by their absence, the bag contained regulation face flannel (Clearly Labelled With Boy's Surname), comb, toothbrush and toothpaste. Except that his mother had forgotten the toothpaste. Mr Malik had noticed this oversight the previous evening but had been much too shy to say anything either to Matron or any of the boys. He simply pretended that there was toothpaste on his brush and hoped that no one noticed. This morning he was feeling a little braver. He would ask that other new boy – Khan – if he could use some of his.

'Help yourself, old boy, it's in the bag.'

So Malik had taken the tube from Khan's sponge bag – a rather smart satiny Pan Am one – applied some paste to his brush and begun scrubbing the old fangs. Hmm, strange toothpaste – not minty. He continued to scrub. Feels funny too – not foamy, greasy. The next moment Mr Malik was leaning over the basin, his mouth afire, spitting for all he was worth. Harry Khan, who had picked up the tube and identified it not as toothpaste but as the ointment he was currently applying three times a day between his toes to cure his athlete's foot, was also doubled up over his basin, not in pain but in mirth. Which attracted all the other boys and the hilarity became general. Which attracted Matron, who dragged poor Malik off to the surgery for a mouthwash with surgical spirit and a stiff precautionary dose of ipecacuanha.

Now, did Harry Khan know or didn't he? He swore to Matron he didn't, and to House. But it hardly mattered, because all the boys assumed he did and thought it a great wheeze.

Then there was the house cricket match. Though Mr Malik had always been very fond of cricket, he couldn't play for toffee. He just didn't seem to be built for it. As he had admitted to Khan, a cricket bat in his hands became a thing with a life of its own, a life dedicated to missing the ball, hitting the stumps or hitting himself. When Mr Malik threw a ball, he had already come to realize, he threw like a girl. If he had a favourite position on the cricket field it was sitting on the pavilion steps with the scorebook on his knees. He was good at that. All those neat and tidy pale blue lines, those dots for runs and nice little symbols for 'bye' and 'wide' and 'not out'. So he was most surprised three weeks into term to find his name up on the board for the house cricket match as player. After two days of agonizing, he finally plucked up courage to question the house captain on his selection.

'Ah yes, heard all about you, Malik. Top scorer at your prep school, I hear. Glad to have you on board.'

'No, House, I . . .'

'Come now, Malik, no need for false modesty. Khan told me all about you. Just what we need.'

'But I . . .'

'Look, don't worry, old chap. I'm sure we're all a bit out of form after the hols. Just turn up in the nets tomorrow after prep and we'll see what you're made of.'

The house captain, he wished to assure Malik the following afternoon after practice, was not angry. He was not angry, he was just very, very disappointed. There was only one way to become a good cricketer, Malik, and that was not by boasting, or lying, or pretending. It was by application. But he was really not angry, and he wanted Malik to treat his one week's double detentions not as a punishment but as a lesson. He would do that, wouldn't he? Malik agreed that he would. On consideration he thought it best not to ask if he might be scorer for the match.

And lastly, there was his nickname. One of the things that Harry Khan was very good at was making up nicknames. He hadn't been at school a term before all the teachers had acquired new nicknames, names which were clever and which stuck. The headmaster Mr Gopal, previously known to both teachers and boys as simply H.M., became The Gop – which was particularly funny if you understood Swahili.

Prakesh Kahdka, who since his infancy had been tall and skinny and known as Stork, became transmuted by Harry Khan into The Stalker, and it became a silly game to run off when he appeared, shouting 'Cheese it – The Stalker', which rather upset poor Prakesh as he was a harmless and friendly soul. As for Mr Malik, he found himself referred to as Jack.

Now you might think that Jack is a harmless enough nick-name. It rolls off the tongue easily enough, and has no obvious link or even rhyme with other words comical or scatological. Even to fluent speakers of Swahili it appears to have no concealed meaning. But it had, and over those long school years Mr Malik grew to hate his nickname and no small part of the pleasure of leaving school to go away to university in London was being able to leave the name behind. When he returned to Kenya two years later he was relieved to find that not only had Harry Khan left Nairobi, the hated nickname seemed to have left with him.

Now Harry Khan was back.

Red-bellied
Tree Duck

5

'Hey, Malik, it *is* you. Long time no see. Lo-o-ong time no see.'

Mr Malik, unsure of what else to do, smiled.

'Hey, I should have guessed – still last in the race. Don't tell me, you took the scenic route?'

Mr Malik's route to the MEATI had been anything but scenic. An overturned matatu on the Langata Road had seen to that.

Harry turned back to the tourists.

'Was Harry right, guys, or was Harry right? Valley Road, way to go. But hey, Malik – you missed a good one.'

'What was it again, Harry?' said one of the tourists, the one with the beard.

'What was it, Rose?' said Harry.

Rose Mbikwa turned towards them. 'A red bishop, Mr Malik,' she said in the accent he so loved. The way she lightly rolled the 'r' in 'red' made him shiver from top to toe. 'A male. Magnificent. I'm sorry you missed it.'

'Yeah,' said Harry, 'it was a beauty.'

Again, Mr Malik smiled. He had long wanted to see the small finch of improbable colour called a red bishop. Ah well, not this time. But at least Harry Khan seemed to have forgotten about 'Jack'.

The Modern East African Tourist Inn – universally known as the MEATI – is well known in Nairobi as *the* place to go to sample local fauna. Where else in Africa – where in the world? – can you see ten species of game roaming wild in an afternoon and eat parts of them that very night? Giraffe, zebra, two or three kinds of antelope, wildebeest, buffalo, crocodile, ostrich, guinea fowl, black duck, they're all on the menu. You won't see many locals eating there. Though most Kenyans love meat few can afford US$60 for just one dinner, and anyway bush food is rather looked down on. Chicken, goat and beef, that's the stuff. Anyone will tell you where to find the MEATI, though, out on Ngong Road just past the old aerodrome.

But the twenty or thirty people gathered outside this tourist restaurant on the edge of the city were not there for the food. They were there because this is one of those transition areas between forest and plains that birds seem to love. The few derelict acres between the restaurant and the barracks of the 1st/2nd Battalion Kenyan Rifle Brigade that lie just down the road have been fenced around with varying degrees of commitment and over the years much rubbish has been dumped there. Not only that but large holes, usually full of water, show where something else has been removed – murram, or clay perhaps. Most of the area is covered with weedy grass and acacias, though a dozen or so bigger trees have somehow survived the axes of the firewood gatherers. The site is on a slight rise and while it is true that if you look south you will see the grassy plains of Nairobi National Park, look north and you have a magnificent view over the Kibera slums. So, not exactly tourist brochure stuff. Rose Mbikwa's voice again cut through the several conversations that had already started up among the group.

'Ah yes. Thank you, Matthew. Soaring above us you have probably all seen the pair of augur buzzards – and as you can see one is the light phase and one the dark phase. And my goodness, is that a blue-headed sunbird?'

All eyes turned to the small jewel of a bird that was sipping nectar from an orange-flowered plant.

'A greenie, I think, Rose,' said Hilary Fotherington-Thomas, squinting down her binoculars.

'Yes, yes,' said Rose. 'A green-headed sunbird. It would, of course, be most unusual to see a blue-headed sunbird this far east. And over here we have a pair of Baglafecht weavers.' She repeated the name. 'Bag-la-fecht weaver. Beautiful.'

'Yeah,' said Harry Khan. 'Almost as beautiful as you, Rose baby.'

'Rose baby?' Mr Malik raised his early morning cup of Nescafé from the table on the veranda and took a slow sip. '*Rose baby?*'

Nearly forty-eight hours had now passed since the bird walk, forty-eight hours in which he had not been able to get those two words out of his head. Mr Malik sighed and put down the cup. He sighed again then, pausing for a moment, picked up the notebook and a pencil that lay beside his two breakfast bananas, as yet untouched. It was the notebook he used for everything, identified on the front cover not with his name but with a rough biro drawing of a black eagle. He leaned forward and recorded a mark at the top of the freshly turned page. That made six so far this morning. A familiar sound made him look up. From behind the yellow banksia rose (his very favourite rose) at the corner of the bungalow came a small figure walking backwards, sweep-sweep-sweeping.

'Ah Benjamin,' said Mr Malik, smiling with sudden inspiration. 'Benjamin, I have a job for you.'

Benjamin, of course, already had a job and he was happy with it. As shamba boy at Number 12 Garden Lane he swept the lawn and swept the paths. Every morning he cut a few branches from whatever tree or bush he thought could best spare them, lashed them to the broom handle with some sisal string, and spent the rest of the day gradually wearing them away on grass and concrete. Once a month he climbed up a ladder on to the roof and swept the gutters. What he swept up he took outside and burned on a bonfire by the side of the road. Every residential street in Nairobi is lined with small bonfires, piled with all the leaves that fall from the trees and other rubbish. The smell of Nairobi is the smell of small bonfires.

Mr Malik showed him the notebook. On the top sheet of paper Benjamin could see drawn a row of sticks.

'I am conducting a survey.' Mr Malik raised the Nescafé to his lips for another inspirational sip. 'A bird survey.'

He put down the cup.

'I would very much like your help. I shall be working at home today. I want you to stay here in the house with me – never mind the sweeping. Now, each time I say the word "hadada" I want you to record it on this piece of paper with this pencil. See? I have already heard, let us see, six hadadas this morning.'

Benjamin propped his broom against the wall, took the pad and counted the marks neatly spaced along the first line of the paper. Mr Malik leaned forward.

'Hadada,' he said, and after a short pause, 'make that two. Mark them down.'

Benjamin drew two sticks on the paper. Mr Malik checked them, nodded, and smiled his approval.

Like Benjamin, you may yourselves well be wondering what nonsense was this. First, you might not know that the hadada is a sort of ibis – a large brown bird with long legs, a long curved beak and a loud voice. Hadadas roost in numbers among the trees in the leafier parts of Nairobi and their eponymous call is one of the more insistent elements of the dawn chorus in that part of the world, though they may be heard at any time of the day. But Mr Malik is not really counting hadadas. He is not really conducting a bird survey. Mr Malik is lying.

And here's a little conundrum: Mr Malik is lying because he is the most honest man in the Asadi Club.

Purple Gallinule

6

Club life in this part of Africa is not all it was. Time was when a fellow, if he were a white fellow, spent half his life at his club. If he lived north of the city it was the Muthaiga Club, if he lived south it was the Karen. Every night after work, and every weekend with the memsahib (and, if they were back from England for the holidays, the children), the club was home from home. But there aren't as many white fellows now in Africa as there used to be – probably even fewer memsahibs – and though anyone white or black can join the Muthaiga or the Karen these days (well, not *anyone*, but you know what I mean) the old clubs are not what they were.

Because that's not where the deals are done. The deals are done in an anonymous white building in the city with black glass in the windows where two large men in tight braided uniforms and sunglasses stand in front of the doors giving small nods to the select few they know are allowed in and ignoring anyone else. The ones they allow in? Very rich, very powerful or very pretty. So where does this leave the Asadi Club? Very nicely, thank you.

For the Asadi Club is where a fellow goes if he is not white or black but brown, and it is where brown men have been going since very soon after they came to Africa from India to help the white men build their railway and stayed to help them build a colony. It is where they still go. The Asadi Club, founded 1903, motto *Spero meliora*, is thriving. Any evening of the week you will find the club car park full of shiny Mercedes and BMWs, the green baize of the four billiard tables (only two at the Muthaiga now, alas) ablur with white and red balls, and empty glasses being exchanged for full ones over the bar as fast as the barmen can pour them. Mr Malik's grandfather was a founding member of the club, his father had been Secretary for nearly forty years, and since Mr Malik's wife died it had become to him a second home. It is where news and gossip is exchanged, and it was where, having spent the day after the bird walk trying to put all thoughts of Harry Khan from his mind and failed utterly, he had gone that evening to find out all there was to know about the man. Patel would know, or Gopez. Which they did, but in finding out what he wanted to know he had also been roped into this 'hadada' business.

'Rot,' said Mr Gopez.

Mr Malik, a glass of cool bedewed Tusker beer in his hand, sat down in the empty chair beside him and reached for the bowl of chilli popcorn.

'Utter piffle.'

Mr Gopez was, he saw, reading the *Evening News*.

'Strong words, A.B., strong words,' murmured Mr Patel from the other side of the table.

'No, really.' Mr Gopez slammed down the paper and picked up his own glass. 'I mean, where do they get this stuff from?'

Mr Patel smiled. He had the delicious feeling there was an argument coming on. Now, was it going to be about something the President had said (always piffle), something the leader-writer had written (almost always piffle), or some item of foreign news (usually to do with the British royal family and usually piffle)? Or, as it was a Wednesday, was it something that chap had written in the 'Birds of a Feather' column (occasionally piffle, but rarely so)? He picked up the discarded paper to find his eye drawn to a small story at the bottom of the page. Danish scientists researching human digestion had, he read, discovered that the average human passes wind one hundred and twenty-three times a day.

'See what I mean?' said Mr Gopez. 'Piffle. Absolute tommyrot. Chap couldn't even fart like that on my mother-in-law's dhal.'

'Oh,' said Mr Patel, 'I don't know.'

Over the many years that he had known Mr A. B. Gopez, Mr Patel had discovered that these four simple words were a sure method to up the ante. With something of the feeling the piece of cheese on a mousetrap might experience as it hears a distant squeak, he awaited his friend's next two words.

'Don't know?' A pair of substantial eyebrows shot ceilingwards. 'Don't know? It stands to bloody reason. Over a hundred farts, that's more than the entire volume of the human body. End of the day, you'd look like a sucked-out samosa. Wouldn't you say, Malik?'

Mr Malik, it must be said, was by now on to his second glass of Tusker with all the recklessness that entails. What he should have said was, 'Hmm.' Instead what he said was, 'Hmm?'

'What do you mean, Hmm?'

'I mean, it might not be quite like that, A.B. A fart, as I understand it, is generated rather than simply stored.'

'Exactly!' said Mr Patel. 'My point entirely. And who knows how big this Danish fart is, eh? Are we talking a delicate little Scandinavian pfff, or the whole raspberry tart?'

'We're talking Standard Danish Farts, we're talking over one hundred a day, and I say it's piffle. Utter tosh.'

This was the moment that Mr Patel had been waiting for.

'And I say it isn't.'

Mr Gopez put down his glass. Giving Mr Malik a look that suggested that their friend was at the least a fool, at the worst an imbecile, he paused. He would try the conciliatory approach.

'Just think about it, Patel, old chap – apply the noggin. One day, twenty-four hours. One hundred and twenty-three farts, that's more than five farts an hour, more than one every twelve minutes. Impossible. As I said, it simply stands to reason.'

'One every eleven minutes and forty-nine seconds, to be exact, A.B. But I don't see that reason has much to do with this – wouldn't you agree, Malik? In cases such as this, the rational approach must surely make way for the empirical.'

Mr Malik said nothing. If he kept silent, there was still a chance.

'What, you're going to count your farts, is it?' The Gopez eyebrows strained for attachment to the Gopez brow. 'And then expect me to believe you? And tell me, in your sleep how do you count farts?'

'Ah,' said Mr Patel. He paused. 'I see what you mean, A.B. Yes, you do have a point.' He paused, as if deep in thought. 'I know,' he said at last. 'Let's ask the Tiger.'

Oh no, thought Mr Malik, not the Tiger.

'Tiger' Singh, club billiard champion, snooker champion, whist champion, badminton champion for eleven years straight until his knee went, was the authority on all things sporting. In the Asadi Club this also encompassed all matters related to betting, both on and off the track. If there was a wager to be made you could rely on the Tiger to calculate the odds, keep the book, and buy beers all round with any profit which accumulated (as it usually seemed to) from his activities. Outside the club he made his living as a lawyer. Called over from the billiard table to hear the case, the Tiger first listened, then spoke.

'Well, gentlemen, *amoto quaeramus seria ludo*, wouldn't you say? Two questions immediately spring to mind. Firstly, how did the Danish fellows do it? Secondly, how much is riding on the result?'

'As for the first question,' said Mr Gopez, pushing the paper towards him, 'I haven't a clue – see for yourself. As for the second . . .' He took wallet from pocket. 'What shall we say, ten thousand?'

This, thought Mr Malik, is getting silly.

Mr Patel also brought out his wallet.

'Ten thousand it is.'

The Tiger held up his hands.

'Wait wait wait, you chaps. Wallets away.' At last someone was seeing sense. 'Before we can even think of making a book we have to decide just what it is we are betting on. Now A.B., exactly what is it you want to wager your ten thousand shillings on?'

'I say – I bet – that these Danish fellows are talking out of their . . . out of their jolly fart-holes. No normal person passes wind more than one hundred times a day.'

'And I,' said Mr Patel, 'say they do.'

'There, simple.'

'Well no, you see A.B., not simple at all,' said the Tiger. 'Clearly, this claim – this hypothesis – needs to be tested. But putting aside for a moment the problem of how we count aforementioned farts – some sort of fancy Danish fart-meter or what? – there is the question of definition. How exactly does one define a fart? *Communi consilio*, as we say in the law. There has to be some agreement, does there not?'

Without waiting for an answer (did I mention he was a lawyer?) the Tiger continued.

'And even more important, how do we verify the result? Who would take whose word for it, if you see what I mean?'

Three brows wrinkled, three pairs of lips pursed.

'If only we had some sort of independent third party . . .' murmured the Tiger.

Three pairs of brown eyes turned as one towards Mr Malik.

Hadada

7

'Hadada.'

Benjamin dutifully made another mark on the paper. Mr Malik, noble Malik, honest Malik, had naturally refused to be any part of the cock-eyed scheme.

'But it's the only way,' said the Tiger.

'No,' said Mr Malik.

'You're the only man,' said Mr Patel.

'No,' said Mr Malik.

'Malik – *clarum et venerabile nomen*.'

'A watchword . . .' said Mr Gopez.

'A byword . . .'

'For honesty . . .'

'For integrity.'

'Wouldn't trust it to anyone else.'

'Couldn't trust it to anyone else.'

'No,' said Mr Malik.

'Honour of the club, old man,' said Tiger Singh.

And that, as they say, did it. Never had a Malik shirked his duty to the Asadi Club. Never had a Malik let down the side.

'Oh, all bloody right,' he said.

Over another round of Tuskers (courtesy of the Tiger, good old Tiger) the rules were agreed, noted, witnessed and signed. Mr Malik would undertake by whatever method he so chose to record the number of gaseous emissions (hereafter referred to as farts) from his lower intestinal orifice over a period of twelve hours, those hours being seven o'clock in the morning until seven o'clock in the evening and the day being the following day. Mr Malik's judgement as to what constituted a true fart would be accepted by all parties and no correspondence would be entered into. It being agreed by all parties impracticable to count farts while asleep, the number of farts in that 12-hour period would be assumed and accepted by all parties to be half of those in any 24-hour period. Mr Malik would report to the Asadi Club at 8 p.m. on the morrow. If the number of farts recorded during the aforementioned 12 hours equalled or exceeded 51, this would be evidence in favour of the Danish claim and Mr Patel would win the bet. If the number of farts equalled or was less than 50, this would be evidence against the Danish claim and Mr Gopez would win the bet. Stakes to be held in trust by H. H. Singh, LLB, MA (Oxon.), barrister-at-law.

The wager had seemed no more sensible when Mr Malik woke up the following morning but there was nothing for it, it had to be done. He reached across the table for his cup of Nescafé.

'Hadada,' he said again.

Benjamin made his fourth mark of the morning, making ten in all. The sudden inspiration to get Benjamin to help in the scheme was a clever stroke, though, thought Mr Malik. Much easier than having to take out his little notebook all the time and mark the damned things down himself, and the boy would enjoy the change from sweeping. And Patel and A.B. had certainly been helpful with all that stuff about Harry Khan. Very helpful. But before we find out what Mr Malik had learned at the Asadi Club about Harry, a little more about Benjamin.

Sixteen years old and never been kissed, Benjamin had been in Mr Malik's employment as shamba boy for only five months. He loved it. Full board and lodging and 350 shillings a month. For the first time in his life he had his own room – a vast echoing room over two metres square, and with a window. And electricity – on, off. And a water tap outside – on, off. And money in his pocket. Of course he sent 250 home, but that left a whopping 100 shillings to spend on . . . on what? On sugar, on bonbons, on Coca-Cola! So much Coca-Cola.

Benjamin had always known how to enjoy life. He was the last in the family, one of those children who in the West are often given the unfortunate label of 'accidents' but in Africa are usually known by more favourable descriptions – in Benjamin's village down in the big valley, such children were referred to as 'late rain'. His nearest brother was seven years older, so Benjamin grew up never lonely but often alone. On his parents' small farm he had enjoyed playing by himself, in dust or mud according to the season. He had enjoyed looking after the chickens, fascinated by the individual character of each bird. He was delighted when he was at last old enough to be sent out with the goats – at first only in the morning, later on all day (though he was slightly disappointed to discover that they were not half as clever as chickens). He loved watching the wild animals – the cheeky mongooses, the tickly scorpions, the shy snakes and lizards, the many kinds of birds coming down to drink at the water tank. He liked talking to the women of the village, and the men, and was overjoyed when at the age of eight, after much deliberation in which it seemed the whole community was involved, he was sent to school. The school was three miles away beside the Nakuru road, so he still had time to throw a stick or climb a tree or watch a bright green snake on the walk there and the walk back. Sometimes he and the other children would climb the big hill behind the school and roll rocks down just for the fun of it, and one time they took an old car tyre up the hill. What a joy it was to see the tyre slowly gather speed then roll and bounce all the way to the bottom. Unlike the rocks, though, the car tyre didn't stop at the bottom of the hill. To the children's glee it kept on bouncing and rolling, across the road, over the fence and onwards. To the children's dismay its forward momentum was only arrested when it slammed into the wall of the school-master's house, causing him to drop the cup of strong tea he habitually brewed to calm himself after classes were finished for the day. But apart from the occasional sore bottom for pranks like this Benjamin enjoyed his schooling and the years went quickly by.

It happened that Benjamin started school soon after the new Minister of Education had issued the decree that school was no longer to be taught in the language of the old colonial masters. Swahili was now to be the lingua franca throughout the country. Benjamin's teacher was a wise man and continued to teach the children English as well as Swahili, and Benjamin enjoyed learning both new languages. He enjoyed it so much that he became the despair of his teacher, always wanting to know the word for this and the word for that. What was the Swahili word for *doguru*, a gang of mongooses? What was the English word for *wakiku*, the little green berries that grew on the kikuya bush? Benjamin's teacher, who had grown up beside Lake Victoria where the local species of mongoose was a solitary animal and wakiku berries were unknown, became so exasperated with his curious pupil that he limited Benjamin (and, to be fair, all the other children) to three questions a day. But this did not stop Benjamin from continuing to ask the questions in his head. Why is a *makari* called a *makari*, why are there different words for male and female *myaki* – *nudzi* and *kiyu* – but not for male and female *hatajii*, and why is there no English word for *huturu* – for surely everyone needs to *huturu*? When Benjamin's schooling finished and he began, aged twelve, to help his father and uncles with the hoeing

34

and the planting in the hasara (or *shamba* as he had now learned to call it in Swahili) Benjamin began to ask them similar questions. His father was a patient man, but after four years of being questioned daily about languages he hardly knew, Benjamin's father (again with the enthusiastic assent of the entire village) packed him off to stay with his mother's younger brother Emanuel in the city.

When Emanuel's boss at the factory where he worked announced that he was in need of someone – trustworthy, efficient, young – who might need a job as shamba boy, Emanuel's arm shot up. After a few more questions to which Emanuel's boss seemed satisfied with the answers – yes this person was young, yes he had worked on the land, yes he was a Christian, and most importantly yes, he had not been long in the city so had not been corrupted by city ways – it was arranged that Benjamin would arrive for an interview the following day at the boss's house.

And as I'm sure you have guessed, Emanuel's boss – proprietor and Managing Director of the Jolly Man Manufacturing Company – was Mr Malik.

Marabou

8

But to get back to what Mr Malik had discovered at the Asadi Club about Harry Khan. The wager business having been arranged, Mr Malik refilled his glass and reached for another handful of chilli popcorn.

'Saw a chap yesterday, haven't seen him in years.'

'Oh really?'

Mr Gopez had picked up the newspaper again and was reading the sports page.

'Yes, not since school.'

'Australia's favourite for the cricket – *again*. What happened to the West Indies? No really, I mean – what happened?'

'Turned up at the bird walk.'

Mr Gopez looked up from his paper.

'The West Indies?'

'No, this chap. Harry Khan.'

'Doesn't sound West Indian.'

'He isn't, he was born here.'

'Are you sure?'

'Yes. I was at school with him.'

'Well, what's he doing playing for the West Indies?'

Mr Malik was rescued by Mr Patel.

'Harry Khan – you mean Bertie Khan's boy?'

'Yes, that's the fellow. As I say, I used to know him at school.'

'Ah,' said Mr Gopez. 'Khan's for Kwality and all that. Died, didn't he?'

'No, I saw him yesterday.'

'Alive?'

'Yes.'

'You're quite sure about that?'

'Yes.'

'Strange. Wonder who got buried then? I'll never forget the samosas. No peas. I don't like peas.'

'I think Malik is talking about Harry Khan, A.B., not Bertie.'

'What, died too, did he?'

'As I recall,' said Mr Patel, 'the family moved to Canada. I heard they did pretty well. Shops and things.'

Tiger Singh broke into the conversation.

'Shops and things, and hotels and things, and import and export and franchises and even a couple of pretty decent restaurants, I heard. Toronto, first, then New York.'

'New York?'

'That's what my wife says. She told me Harry Khan was back in town. Fourth wife just divorced him – serial adultery according to my wife. A philanderer of the first water, she says – none of this no-fault nonsense with her. Looking for another one I suppose.'

Another wife? No, please, no. Not Harry Khan. Not . . . Rose. And not when Mr Malik had just written that letter.

The letter. I'm sure you remember that Mr Malik is rather enamoured of Rose Mbikwa – indeed, if you were to use the word 'enraptured' or even 'entranced' you might be nearer the mark. He had fallen for her the moment he first saw her, and three years of seeing the woman of his dreams at each Tuesday morning bird walk had only fuelled the flames of his passion. You may have gathered that Mr Malik is not a brash, confident, outgoing kind of chap. But you have also discovered that when the chips are down, he is by no means a cowardly man. Put these facts together with the imminent occurrence of the premier social occasion of the Kenyan calendar, and what you get is Mr Malik sitting down at his desk the previous week (immediately after the bird walk, as it happens) to pen a letter to Mrs Rose Mbikwa in which he asked whether she would do him the honour of accepting his invitation to accompany him to the annual Nairobi Hunt Club Ball.

Mr Malik, it has to be said, is not a dancer. I am not a runner – running just doesn't feel right. But in my dreams I am Pheidippides running fleet of foot from Marathon to Athens to announce victory over the Persians; I am Tom Longboat at Madison Square Garden breaking the line three full minutes ahead of the pack; I am Julius Ruto. In his dreams Mr Malik is Fred Astaire, and not only did he write this letter inviting Rose Mbikwa to the ball, he put it into an envelope, addressed it and stamped it. Though he was not yet in possession of a single ticket to the ball – let alone two – he had already sent a confident cheque and as soon as the tickets arrived he would walk down to the postbox on the corner of Garden Lane and Parklands Drive and post that letter.

Think back to when you were younger. Think of that letter (or email, or text message if you must) to that someone. Think of waiting for the reply. Would Rose accept? Of course not. No, of course not. A reply would arrive, an exquisite little note in a stiff paper envelope. Extremely polite, no reasons given. But might she? Well, she might. The phone would ring and he would say, 'Malik here,' and he would hear her say that it was a perfectly lovely idea and she hadn't been to the Hunt Club Ball for years and she would love to come. Or he would be out and when he got home there would be a message on the pad – no name, just one word. Yes.

A word about the Nairobi Hunt. Had you been outside the main entrance to the Karen Club early on the morning of the last Saturday in May of 1962, you would have seen assembled on the lawn seventeen horses and riders – red jackets, white jodhpurs, black riding hats and all. A cacophony of bays and barks announces the arrival of a full pack of foxhounds, brought from the kennels just down the road past the tennis courts. As the first rays of sun peep over the Ngombo Hills, the final meeting of the Nairobi Hunt rides out. Before the morning is over they will have found and killed two foxes, which was two more than usual, and the hunt is judged a great success. It is a fitting finale to a tradition which has been going on for more than fifty years.

I should explain that the foxes were really jackals – there being no suitable foxes in that part of Africa – but they were always called foxes by members of the hunt. The foxhounds were real foxhounds, though – descendants of those brought over by Lord Delamere of blessed memory in 1912. But while all the hounds have long since passed over to that great hunting ground in the sky, and galloping over the dewy savannah towards the rising sun trying to spot the aardvark holes while taking a stiff pull from the whisky flask is now but a fading memory in the minds of a few Old Hands, the hunt has not completely vanished. Its ghost still exists as the Hunt Committee of the Karen Club, whose sole function is to arrange the annual Hunt Club Ball. Come, let me take you there.

We are in the Grand Ballroom of the Suffolk Hotel. Chandeliers sparkle, the candles are lit. Swathes of bougainvillea wreathe the columns along each side of the room, whole branches of hibiscus adorn windows and doors. At the far end of the room the orchestra is tuning up. Tonight, just as on this night for the last twenty-nine years, we will thrill to the music of Milton Kapriadis and his Safari Swingers. Along one side of the room the starched white cloth of the long table is almost hidden beneath scores of laden plates and dishes.

The buffet consists, as usual, of assorted canapés (I see vol-au-vents are big again this year), followed by salads, cold meats, devilled chicken and devilled shrimps, curries, birianis, fruit platters, and cakes that would have made my grandmother – who had a thing for pink icing and whipped cream – cry. On a separate table, watched over by a white-uniformed and tall-hatted chef with carving implements agleam, rests a whole roasted sheep. Two more are ready in the kitchen waiting to be brought out – they have always done these things well at the Suffolk. Teams of waiters, white-saronged, maroon-jacketed and silver-buttoned, stand beside the door, silver trays balanced on white-gloved hands. On each tray are two glasses each of beer, gin and tonic, whisky soda, brandy soda, and plain soda water – the 'big five' drinks of East Africa. So, let the party begin.

Who will be arriving at the ball? Well, everybody, really. Two hundred couples and more of the very top layers of Kenyan Society. All the Old Hands, of course, and most of the Young Hands, and quite a few of their brattish offspring – most of whom have abandoned Africa for Kensington or Belgravia (or even Islington these days) but still return once a year to avoid the British winter. It is a tradition that the British High Commissioner attend the ball, and (apart from a three-year hiatus during Harold Macmillan's leadership in the UK when the winds of change sweeping through Africa put a chill on such frivolities), he usually does. There is also a fair smattering of other high-ups from the rest of the diplomatic community and the various NGOs that nowadays have made a home in Nairobi.

The band strikes up, the British High Commissioner and his wife take the floor for the first waltz (it is always a waltz, the British High Commissioner is always a man, and he is always married), and off we go. Dancing, chatting, eating, drinking, flirting – and above all, being seen. I've been there, and it really is quite fun. Mr Malik, whose wife had never been keen on all this old colonial stuff and nonsense, had not been there and was not sure if it would be fun, but he knew that it was the only place that he wanted to take Rose Mbikwa. The tickets might well arrive in the very next post.

As soon as they did, his invitation was ready to pop into the postbox at the corner of Garden Lane and Parklands Drive.

Sunbird

9

At her home in Serengeti Gardens, Hatton Rise, Rose Mbikwa was standing in her bedroom, an empty suitcase on the bed. As she had explained at the bird walk that morning, she would be away next week. What she had not explained was why.

I have already mentioned that the car Rose drives is a Peugeot 504 and that it has seen better days. But though the last 504 came off the Sausheim production line in 1989 they're tough old cars – thousands are still found on African roads from Cape Town to Cairo. The 1600cc engine, basically the same unit that was used in the old Pinafarina-styled 404, just seems to keep chugging on for ever. The four-speed manual gearbox, while lacking top-end speed, is legendary for its reliability. What usually goes first is the differential, though the decline is gradual and the whine of a worn-out worm gear can accompany a Peugeot 504 for years before it finally gives up its mechanical ghost.

So it is with many a human body. As the years roll on there is often one part that starts to show signs of wear before the others. With Rose, apart from that occasional twinge in her left hip after a particularly strenuous walk, it was not engine or transmission that was the problem, though. It was her eyes.

At first she tried to ignore the slight fuzziness that seemed to surround things, especially in bright light. It was nothing serious, it would get better by itself. It didn't. Oh well, just getting old – perhaps some glasses would fix it, the ones you can get at the pharmacist should do. They didn't. As her eyesight got worse she noticed that her colour vision was being affected (fancy mistaking that green-headed sunbird for a blue-headed). She went to see her doctor and told him all about it. He looked closely into each of her eyes down an ancient ophthalmoscope.

'I regret to say, Mrs Mbikwa, that you are developing cataracts. The one in the lens of your left eye is particularly bad. It's going yellow, which is probably why you are having trouble with some colours.'

The doctor explained that the condition was particularly common in his white patients.

'All this strong light and infrared, you know. It damages the proteins. I'm afraid it will only get worse.'

He recommended that she should consider a lens replacement.

'Just the left one to start with. It's a simple enough procedure and the lenses are very reliable these days, though I have to say it's not the kind of thing we're very good at here in Kenya.'

He suggested she have the operation somewhere in Europe or the US.

The news, though half suspected, was devastating. Of all the things to fail, her eyesight was the most difficult to cope with. What about her guide training? What about the bird walks? Could she even live without the beauty of her beloved birds? But there, nothing could be done. There was no way Rose was going to spend that kind of money on herself even if she could somehow scrape it together, and what cannot be cured must be endured. She thanked her doctor and went home. Her vision got worse. But then just last month her son Angus, now grown-up and graduated and working for the United Nations, was visiting from Geneva. He soon saw through his mother's stoic pretence. He made a few phone calls.

'You're booked in at Dr Strauss's clinic in Bonstetten next Wednesday. I've arranged the air tickets. Don't argue, Mother dear, it's all paid for.'

So that very afternoon Rose is due to leave on the Swiss International flight to Zurich. She will be away for nine days. While she looks around the bedroom, deciding what to pack and what to leave behind, let us examine the rest of the house.

Hatton Rise was built in the 1920s as a comfortable middle-class suburb for white settlers. Think Sunningdale in Berkshire or some of the older parts of Freeport, Long Island and you will have some idea of its comfortable houses in spacious grounds. It is now an upper-class suburb for Kenyans of any colour who can afford a house there. Rose has lived in the house on the hill in Serengeti Gardens ever since she was married. She is now the only white person in the street. On the side where Bunny and Sue Harrington used to live, her neighbour is now an Asian businessman who owns the Coca-Cola bottling plant in Nairobi, the largest in East Africa (Rose seldom sees his wife). On the other side – a sprawling hacienda-style building that once housed the younger Delamere boy, his good friend Jeremy and at least a dozen dachshunds – now lives a justice of the high court who, judging by the ever-changing number and variety of cars always jamming the driveway and spilling out into the street, has a surfeit of disposable income and a small problem with brand loyalty.

Though Rose's is a large house it is, by modern East African standards, old-fashioned. The rooms are not small, but nor are they as palatial as the newer houses in the street. Downstairs the main sitting room opens on to a veranda through folding wooden doors. Folding in theory, that is; it has been many years since anyone thought to close them and it is doubtful now whether the hinges would stand it. The veranda extends the full width of the back of the house, and sometimes Rose sits outside on the rattan chairs under the yellow banksia rose (her very favourite rose) and sometimes she sits inside on one or other of the old armchairs or lies back on the sofa. She isn't like some people, with 'their' chair. There is a music system in the corner with a jumble of wires behind it and CDs in untidy stacks on the shelves above, but no television and so no enormous satellite dish in the garden – a feature of most homes in the street these days. Neither is there air conditioning. Even if Rose liked air conditioning, with the veranda door in the shape it's in there would not be much point. Adjoining the sitting room but separated by three archways is the dining room, with its large walnut table, twelve chairs and matching sideboard. Made in Dundee in the early nineteenth century, they were a late wedding present from her father. The kitchen is off the dining room and there is a cloak-room in the entrance hall by the front door. A stairway leads off the entrance hall to four plain, square bedrooms upstairs and a bathroom. Yes, only one bathroom. That's how old-fashioned it is.

A feature of Rose's home is the number of photographs and pictures that crowd every wall. Over the mantelpiece in the sitting room (there is a wide fireplace in the sitting room, though she seldom uses it these days) is a portrait in oils of a handsome black man in a grey pinstripe suit. He is sitting at a desk with a sheet of paper before him and a fountain pen in his hand. The shelves behind him are lined with books bound in black and red, giving the impression that this man is serious, important – a lawyer or a politician perhaps. The impression is slightly spoilt by the fact that the man wears a large and cheerful grin. This is Joshua Mbikwa, the man who thirty-five years ago swept the young Rose Macdonald off her Scottish feet. This is the man who introduced her to Africa. This is the man she still loves.

Rose clicked closed the locks on the old Samsonite suitcase, picked up the phone and dialled. She would accept that invitation of a lift after all. It would save the bother of having to find a taxi. At only the fifth attempt she got through to the Hilton and was connected to the room of Harry Khan.

Tiger Singh and A.B. had been quite right about Harry. His grandfather Mohammed Khan had first come to Africa from India for the same reason as most of his compatriots – to build the railway for the British. The British had decided that they couldn't do it themselves (white labourers couldn't take the heat, you see) but had soon discovered that the local African men saw no reason to labour all day for a bowl of rice when they could sit under a tree for the same length of time and be brought a bowl of sorghum by their womenfolk. So the British recruited shiploads of Indian labourers, each of whom as he came down the gangplank at Mombasa was handed a shovel and a bowl, and they got that railway built quicksmart (even despite the delays caused by those man-eating lions which everyone still makes such a fuss about). But when on 16th July 1903 the first train puffed along that railway all the way from the Indian Ocean to Lake Victoria, what was Harry Khan's grandfather to do then – go back to the dustbowl that was central India and be bossed around by the British some more? Mohammed Khan had already noticed that there might be openings for a man with get-up-and-go in this strange but fertile country. Though he had started out on the railway with a shovel in his hand just like everyone else, he had soon risen to become at first foreman, then section boss, then line supply manager. He still worked long hours, but his promotion meant that he travelled up and down the line and had a little time to look around. In one section the engineers were being delayed by a shortage of dynamite.

Down in Mombasa, in a little tin shed with a padlock on the door, he happened to know that stacked against the wall were several cases of dynamite left over from when the harbour master had conceived a grand plan to extend the harbour wall with coral rock blasted from a nearby hill. Two loud bangs were enough to show the harbour master that the rock was so fragile the shock from blasting reduced it to useless dust, and the dynamite still sat in its Swedish pine boxes in this small tin shed down by the wharf. Mohammed Khan introduced the harbour master to the chief railway engineer and a deal was struck. For his trouble the harbour master thanked Harry Khan's grandfather with the first thing that came to hand, which happened to be several bolts of bright red Manchester worsted that had been left at his office, in mysterious circumstances, by the owner of a private steam yacht.

Mohammed Khan gratefully accepted the red cloth from the harbour master and had an inspiration. He cut it up into lengths and on his next Saturday off, took his merchandise up the line to sell at the market behind the station in Nairobi. The first Saturday he sold one square of cloth to a passing Maasai. The second Saturday he sold twenty, the third a hundred. Almost every passing Maasai goat and cattle herder – and many Maasai did pass by the railway station, drawn there by its strange spectacle – decided that he would like a new red cloak. Thus it was that the Maasai, who had until then favoured cloth the colour of the earth they walked, acquired their taste for red cloaks which continues to this day, and thus it was that Mohammed Khan first went into trade.

By the time old Mohammed was ready to pass on the business to his son it had become one of the largest trading houses in East Africa. Advertisements extolling 'Khan's for Kwality' could be seen from the boat jetty at Mombasa to the railway terminus at Entebbe, from the plains of Serengeti almost to the very peak of Kilimanjaro.

Harry's father had gone on to consolidate this small empire of trade, and by the 1960s the family was one of the richest in East Africa. But then things went bad. Independence was coming, business confidence went belly up. Unrest and unruliness spread across Kenya; tribes called for tribalization, nationalists for nationalization. As soon as Harry, the youngest of the children, finished his schooling at Eastlands High, the Khans sold up, packed their bags, and moved to Toronto.

They did well there and expanded operations into the US. Harry had by now joined the family firm but his part was mainly 'front of house'. He had no head for figures like his brother Aladin, no eye for a business bargain like his brother Salaman, but he had a gift. He could make people feel good. When a new hotel was being opened, Harry was the one who arranged the party, greeted the guests and made the speeches. When finance was being sought for a new shopping centre, Harry was the one who took the bankers to lunch. When a franchise was being sold, he was the one who entertained the franchisees' wives (they did like Harry, those franchisees' wives).

Meanwhile his elder brothers made the deals and counted the money, of which there was always enough so that they seldom had to question Harry about his credit cards and charge accounts. He began keeping an uptown apartment in Toronto overlooking the St Lawrence and a downtown apartment in Manhattan over-looking the East River. He was now on to his fifth apartment in both cities, each of his previous wives having claimed one, and he was getting bored. And his brothers were getting exasperated; so many wives, no children. Perhaps, they suggested, he needed to get away. It would be hard, but they would manage without him for a few weeks – a few months even. What about a visit to the old country? (Yes, they were pretty sure you could use Amex in Africa.) Maybe Mom would like to go too, eh? And he could scout around. There might be some good business opportunities again in East Africa these days – franchises, perhaps? Harry agreed.

Exactly how he would spend the three months there he had no idea, but he was sure something would turn up.

Paradise
Flycatcher

10

In the forty-four years that had passed since Harry Khan and his mother had last driven along the road that leads from the international airport to the city of Nairobi, much had changed. Harry didn't recognize it at all. His mother, sitting in the back of the nice new Range Rover in which her nephew Ali had met them, kept shaking her head as she thought she recognized some long-forgotten landmark of yesteryear, now hemmed in with stark concrete office buildings and car and furniture showrooms. 'Aieiii,' she would say. On the whole trip into town – past the football stadium, past Uhuru Park, the new parliament building, the old university – that is all she said. Aieiii.

'I don't remember any of these street names,' said Harry.

'They changed them all, old boy,' said his cousin. 'We're postcolonial now, don't you know.'

Turning right off the Uhuru Road (Queen's Avenue) he drove them down Kenyatta Parade (Prince's Street), past a petrol station and left at a small roundabout where half a dozen young boys dressed in rags watched with vacant eyes. The large car bumped along a potholed lane for a couple of hundred metres, then turned into a gateway on which was mounted, in shining gold letters, the words 'Sea Spray'.

'And I certainly don't remember this.'

'It's new. Quieter than the Hilton. I thought it would be better for Auntie.'

'What about the old Livingstone?'

'Ah, you mean The Dawn of Africa. Under new management.' Ali shook his head. 'Not what it was.'

Harry had no need to ask why they were not staying at the Stanley. No Khan had set foot in the Stanley since the day fifty years ago when his father, on the way to the dining room for lunch with an important client, had been mistaken by the manager for a waiter and threatened with the sack if he didn't chop-chop. But the Sea Spray (only its owners, a Saudi Arabian family who have never set foot in it, know why a hotel approximately two hundred and fifty miles from the nearest ocean is so called) looked like a fine modern hotel. They checked in, Harry's mother found her room and retired to bed while Harry and Ali retired to the bar.

It had been arranged that the three of them would stay for just one night in Nairobi before driving on in the morning to Naivasha. Ali still kept the large house on the lake that their grandfather had built there as his country retreat in the thirties, and where the Kenyan and American branches of the family had agreed that it would be good for Harry's mother to stay during her three months in Kenya. It would be easier to have the relatives visit her rather than travelling around to meet all of them. This proved a wise decision. The sooner they got out of this ruined city, she informed her son and nephew at breakfast the next morning, the happier she would be.

The house at Naivasha had changed little. Still the long euphorbia hedge lining the road, still the tall iron gates opening on to the long murram drive, still the wide lawns and flamingo-pink stucco of the house itself. Harry's mother loved it; Harry did not. He was bored. So three days later, after making sure that his mother had settled back into life in Africa and was already so used to having servants again that she was quite back to her bossy old ways, Harry Khan was only too happy to accept the invitation of his cousin's wife's sister's youngest daughter Elvira – the spoilt one, the pretty one, the unmarried-but-engaged one who had been down to visit her auntie – to head back to the city for a few days. Her fiancé, an accountant of good family and serious intent, was unfortunately working in Dubai but she would be delighted to show Harry around the town.

This time he booked into the Hilton. He hired a red Mercedes. Elvira showed him as much as she could of the city's charms and more than she should of her own and everywhere took American Express. This wasn't so bad after all, thought Harry. Then the fiancé arrived back in town.

And so it was that Harry Khan, bored now in the city and at a loose end, found himself one morning walking over to the museum (of all places) to while away a few hours before his head was clear enough to motor over to a restaurant he had heard about just outside town for a couple of beers and a bit of lunch. And so it was that he met Rose Mbikwa.

This is how Rose fills her week. Monday morning, staff meeting. That is to say her own domestic staff, of whom she employs five – Elizabeth the housekeeper, Reuben the 63-year-old gardener (she refuses to call him 'shamba boy') and three askaris, Mokiya, old Mukhisa and young Mukhisa, to guard the house and gate in Serengeti Gardens. She doesn't really need all these staff. Rose is a competent cook and enthusiastic gardener. Nor does she feel she needs guarding. The high walls, razor-wire fences and elaborate alarm systems favoured by so many of her neighbours would make her feel more threatened than safe (and besides, Rose knows that if they really want to get you, they will). But her house had been built with generous servant accommodation, and it would be wrong not to have it used, just as it would be wrong not to give honest employment when so many people have none. She was one of the lucky ones and, as Joshua used to say, it is good to share your luck around. Since coming to work for Rose all three askaris – young Mukhisa in particular – have become keen birdwatchers and are forever calling her outside to observe, and sometimes identify, an especially lovely or unusual bird.

Monday afternoon is given over to correspondence. Tuesday morning, bird walk; Tuesday afternoon, working at the museum on the guide training project – ditto all Wednesday and Thursday. On Friday morning Rose usually does a stint as volunteer guide at the museum itself, leaving the afternoon free for the weekly shopping, with Elizabeth to help with the bargaining and Reuben to help with the carrying. That particular Friday morning she was about to lead a party of tourists up the main staircase to the Joy Adamson gallery when she noticed a well-dressed man loitering on the edge of the group. When he caught her eye she smiled.

'Please, you are welcome to join us.'

Over the next hour and a half Harry Khan learned more about Kenya than he had picked up in all the eighteen years he had lived there, especially about the birds. Imagine, over a thousand different species – more than in the whole of North America. By the time the tour was over he was really beginning to believe that the land of his birth was quite a special place. As he was about to leave there was a crash of thunder and the heavens opened. There was no point in walking back to the hotel and getting soaked, but should he wait till it passed or should he get a taxi? There must be a taxi rank somewhere nearby. At that moment the tall white woman appeared, umbrella in hand.

'Could you tell me where I can find a cab?' said Harry. 'And thanks for the talk.'

'You can usually find one just outside the gate. And thank you, I'm glad you enjoyed it.'

Rose recognized him as the white-haired Indian man who had tagged on to the tour. He was quite good-looking, she had thought, in a flashy kind of way – and was that an American accent? She asked him where he was going, he said the Hilton, she said she could give him a lift. He asked her in for a cup of coffee, she accepted. And she'd really enjoyed herself. It was, she couldn't help thinking as she found herself spluttering into her cup of coffee after another of Harry's outrageous stories about an American franchisee's wife (complete with Midwestern accent), a long time since she had laughed like this. When he had asked her whether she would like to have lunch with him – he'd heard about this restaurant just outside town – she found herself saying yes (well, why not, and anyway if they sat outside there were bound to be a few birds to look at). So she went to lunch with him at Tusks, and as well as hearing more funny stories she was surprised to find that he'd shown a lot of interest in the birds too. The sight of a male paradise flycatcher with glowing chestnut tail perched on a jacaranda just metres from the veranda where they ate their lunch had quite entranced him. So when Harry said let's do this again – how about dinner tomorrow night at the Hilton? – she'd said yes without even thinking about it.

And that's when they'd danced.

Buzzard

II

'What do men want from women?' my grandmother asked me one day apropos of nothing at all as we waited to be served at the off-sales counter of the Crown and Anchor, one of the several public houses which were favoured in strict rotation as provendors of the daily bottle of sweet sherry she so enjoyed. Without waiting for an answer she said in a loud voice, 'Sex.' Satisfied with the look she had created on my late adolescent features, she continued.

'And what do women want from men?'

I shook an embarrassed head.

'A good dancer.'

There is, I have come to realize as I have grown older and fonder of sweet sherry, much in this. I suspect it is a sentiment with which Rose Mbikwa would concur. Rose loves to dance.

Think back to the spring of 1959. We still have twelve months to go until Mr Chubby Checker introduces the twist to the world. We will have to wait another twenty-four before Ray Barretto's

'El Watusi' starts yet another planet-wide dance craze. From Burbank to the Bronx, from Spain to Scotland, rock and roll is still king of the charts and undisputed ruler of the dance floor, and in the junior common room of Edinburgh Presbyterian Ladies' College fourteen-year-old Rose Macdonald is rocking and rolling with the best of them – the best of them in this case being her fellow pupils at the exclusive Edinburgh girls' school still noted for producing the crème de la crème. See them step, see them pass, see them do the sugar push. When Elvis curls that lip from the black and white Decca TV in the corner of the room, see the girls all swoon. Oh yeah, hit that rhythm eight to the bar and make it fast, daddy-o. By the time Rose Macdonald had moved on from school to university the rhythm may have changed to 4/4 and the habit of actually touching your partner as you danced may have been temporarily suspended, but she never forgot the exhilaration of those first dances and she never forgot the steps. At the Nairobi Hilton with Harry Khan that first Saturday evening after they met, she found that Harry hadn't forgotten them either.

Later that evening, as she left the hotel to drive home, she said, 'See you at the bird walk on Tuesday?'

'You know, Mrs Mbikwa,' said Harry, 'I think you will.'

At precisely 8 p.m. on the following Thursday – which is to say two days after the bird walk, two days after *Rose baby*, and the day after the fart bet – Mr Malik walked into the packed bar of the Asadi Club. In his right hand was a black leather briefcase. Messrs Gopez, Patel and Singh, seated together at a table near the bar, looked up as he came in but said nothing. He sat down in the empty chair beside them, opened the briefcase and took from within it a simple notebook. Without comment, he passed it to the Tiger.

'So, Malik,' said the Tiger, putting the notebook, unopened, on the table before him. 'You have completed your task?'

Mr Malik nodded.

'And the results of your investigation are in this book?'

'They are.'

'Were you able to satisfactorily carry out the procedure, as stipulated in the agreement here drawn up and witnessed last night, in verification of the wager between the two members of the Asadi Club now before us?'

'I was.'

'Gentlemen.' As the Tiger rose to his feet a hush fell. 'Gentlemen, you have heard the words of our noble friend Malik. Before I open this book and declare the winner of the bet, does either of you' – he turned to face the protagonists – 'have anything to say regarding the agreement, the procedure, or any matter pertaining thereunto?'

First Mr Gopez then Mr Patel shook their heads. The Tiger let his eyes traverse the still silent room.

'Does any member of the Asadi Club here present have anything to say vis-à-vis or pertaining to this matter – namely the wager between these two gentlemen, Mr Gopez and Mr Patel?'

Ignoring a muffled and slightly slurred 'Yes, get on with it' from a voice at the back of the room (Sanjay Bashu, no doubt), the Tiger removed a pair of half-spectacles from his shirt pocket and adjusted them on his nose.

'Gentlemen, I have the figure before me. *Ad utrumque paratus.*' He opened the book, his eyebrows lifting in a millimetre of apparent surprise. 'You will recall that if this figure equals or exceeds fifty-one, the wager will go to Mr Patel. If it equals or is less than fifty, Mr Gopez will win the bet. The figure, gentlemen, is . . .'

Once more his eyes swept round the silent barroom.

'. . . forty-two.'

There was a moment in which you could have heard a distant flea fart, then a cacophony of groans mingled with an equal number of whoops and cheers. A. B. Gopez stood and reached across the table. Mr Patel, with only the hint of a scowl, shook the proffered hand. Over the hubbub of excited voices the Tiger shouted to the bar.

'Four Tuskers. And four Johnnie Walkers too – large ones.'

There were calls for a recount – not from Mr Patel, who had already accepted defeat like the true clubman he was, but from one or two younger members. Mr Malik's book, which had been making the rounds of the bar for inspection, was duly found and returned to the Tiger, whose forensic skill did not take long to spot that ten additional marks had been made with ink of a slightly different colour. He tossed the appeal out of court with stern warnings of the penalties for contempt.

Mr Malik had just begun explaining to Patel and A.B. how he had used the services of his shamba boy to help with the count, when Harry Khan walked into the bar.

Cormorant

12

Had the great god Ganesha himself walked into the barroom of the Asadi Club at that moment – four-armed, elephant-headed, broken-tusked and crowned with diamonds – Mr Malik could not have been more surprised. But there, all white and smiling, was Harry Khan. Thick white hair, a shirt almost as dazzling as his teeth, white trousers, white jacket and (yes, the man has no shame) white patent pumps. And on his arm, dressed in a very short red dress, a very pretty young woman.

The Asadi Club when first set up in 1903 was simply a club for Indians. Anyone from the subcontinent could apply for membership, regardless of race or religion – it said so in the club rules. In practice this meant that there were no women members, because whoever heard of a woman wanting to join a club? It was only after the embarrassment of what later became known as the 'Ranamurka Affair' of 1936 that the club rules were amended to deliberately exclude women. So things remained until the mid-seventies, when the new wave of feminism (somewhat delayed and diluted among the Asian community of Nairobi but nonetheless detectable) coincided with a decline in club membership. After much debate – and despite the threat of Jumbo Wickramasinghe to shoot the first female member to cross the threshold of the club, then shoot himself – women were allowed to join. But as no effort was made to attract them – how many women really want to play billiards and drink beer all night, and have you seen the Ladies loo? – immediate bloodshed was averted. Still, some thirty years later, almost the only time you saw women at the club was when wives and daughters turned up for the regular first-Sunday-of-the-month curry tiffin. On a weekday night – never.

All eyes turned to the young woman on Harry Khan's arm. She was, as I'm sure you will have guessed, his cousin's wife's sister's youngest daughter Elvira – the spoilt one, the pretty one, the unmarried-but-engaged one, who as soon as her fiancé had flown back to Dubai had immediately rung up Uncle Harry to see if he wanted to do something. After they'd done something he said he'd like a drink and she said she was bored with the stuffy old Hilton and that her brother Sanjay was bound to be at the club so why not go there for a drink instead. It would be a lark.

Her brother (the same Sanjay Bashu who had interjected from the bar not half an hour before and had since been dosing his disappointment after backing Patel to win the fart bet with liberal doses of J. Walker's internal embrocation) assured her that he was happy to see her.

'No, I mean really happy, Wee Wee. I mean that, I really do. Very, very happy.'

Harry moved towards the bar, leaving his pretty niece to remind her inebriated sibling in forceful whispers not to call her by that silly name any more and that if he did it one more time then she might be forced to recount a certain story about a certain pet hyrax. At a table by the bar he saw four men, three staring towards him, one staring pointedly away. He recognized only one of them.

'Malik, great to see you again!'

There was nothing Mr Malik could do, nowhere he could go. He turned towards Harry Khan, gave a polite smile and took the hand that had been thrust towards him.

'Ah, Harry.'

Patel, A.B. and the Tiger were impressed and intrigued. Impressed, because the girl, having apparently finished giving Sanjay Bashu a piece of her mind, was now sashaying towards them in a dress of a cut and lack of covering-power seldom seen in Nairobi, let alone the Asadi Club. And intrigued because this was the Harry Khan that Malik had been so interested in, was it?

'Great place,' said Harry, flashing his whitest smile. 'Love it. This is where you hang out, eh Malik? Wondered why I hadn't seen you at the Hilton. Have you met my niece? Elvira, meet my old friend Malik. We were at school together.'

More handshakes.

'Hey, Malik, what was it we used to call you?'

'Call me?'

'Yeah, you know – at school.'

'At school?' Mr Malik felt the sweat break out cold on his brow. 'I don't remember. Let me introduce you to . . .'

'Mack, that was it. No.' Harry looked towards the ceiling for inspiration. 'Damn. Never mind, it'll come back to me. Who did you say your friends were?'

After further introductions were made, drinks ordered and a few questions answered about what had brought Harry here and how was his mother, Mr Patel turned with an innocent smile to Elvira.

'I don't suppose you're interested in birds, at all?' And appearing to take her silence as assent, 'You must get Malik here to tell you about his hadadas.'

Mr Malik was about to leap in with a statement firmly ornithological when Harry beat him to it.

'Birds, sweetness,' he said. 'Big brown birds. I've been finding out a lot about birds this past weekend, you know.'

And Mr Malik's annoyance at his friend Patel's mischievous attempt to embarrass him was immediately replaced by another feeling altogether.

Birds? Where? With whom?

'You guys met Rose Mbikwa?' continued Harry. 'What she doesn't know about our feathered friends. Did you know you can see two hundred kinds of birds just in Nairobi? And boy, can she dance.'

Dance? *Dance?*

Red Bishop

13

'Dance?' said Mr Malik. Rose Mbikwa – with Harry Khan?

'Yeah, dance. Rock and roll. Man can that pussycat swing. You know that jukebox at the Hilton? One of the really old ones and music to match. Bill Haley, Little Richard, even the Big Bopper himself. Hey, maybe I should ask her to that dance here – what did you say it was called again, honey?'

'You mean the Hunt Club Ball, Uncle Harry?'

'Yeah, the Hunt Club Ball. Know where I can get a couple of tickets?'

'You can't.' Mr Malik hadn't meant to say it. The words just seemed to come out. 'All gone, sold out. Anyway, you have to be a member.'

'Member of what?' said Mr Patel.

'The club. Karen Club. So I've heard.'

'Nonsense, old man,' said Mr Patel. 'I've been to it myself.'

'Ah . . . but they're probably all allocated. Isn't that right, Tiger?'

Though the Tiger had not the slightest idea what was going on he could not ignore the beseeching look on the face of his friend.

'Er, yes, well, quite possibly. If you say so, Malik old chap.'

'Oh don't worry, Uncle. Sanjay will give you his. I'm sure he will if I ask him nicely.'

It seemed that Elvira's brother Sanjay had already ordered four tickets and her fiancé had promised to come back from Dubai for the weekend to take her. There was nothing else for it.

'Anyway,' said Mr Malik, 'you can't ask Mrs Mbikwa.'

'Why the hell not?' said Harry.

'You can't,' said Mr Malik, 'because I have written her an invitation myself.'

It was Mr Patel who voiced the question that had simultaneously sprung into the heads of each person around the table.

'You?'

Mr Malik nodded.

It was Mr Gopez who asked the next question.

'What did she say?'

'She . . .' Mr Malik was almost going to say that she hadn't replied. For nine days the invitation to Rose had been his secret alone, and for nine days a small flame of hope had burned in his heart. It was unlikely, but it was possible – just possible – that she would accept. All he had to do was get the tickets, then post the invitation. But now the secret was out the whole thing was revealed to him as what he feared it had been all along. It was a joke, a pathetic hopeless joke. And he, Malik, was a bigger joke. But despite the looks on the faces now before him, still that small flame was not quite extinguished. There was something inside him, something deep in his heart, that assured Mr Malik his invitation to Rose Mbikwa to accompany him to the Hunt Club Ball was not a joke at all. It was a sincere offer, it was a compliment honestly given, and no matter what anyone else might think Rose Mbikwa would know this.

'I haven't posted it yet.'

A moment's silence was followed by a whoop from Harry Khan.

'Haven't posted it? What kind of invitation is that?'

'I just haven't . . . haven't got round to it yet. It's all ready, though. And I've ordered the tickets.'

'Let me get this right,' said Harry. 'You haven't got a ticket, and you haven't sent the invitation.'

'Yes, but . . .'

'Save your stamp, Malik. I'm phoning her right now.'

It was the Tiger who spoke.

'Before any telephone calls are made or letters posted, gentlemen, a moment's reflection might be appropriate.'

'What's to reflect?' said Harry. 'All's fair in love and dancing – right, guys?'

'There is some truth in what you say, Mr Khan,' said the Tiger. 'But Malik does seem to have some claim to priority here.'

'I don't see what the problem is,' said Mr Gopez. 'Why can't both of them invite her?'

'Because, A.B., that would put the lady in a very tricky position. *A fronte praecipitium a tergo lupi*, if you see what I mean. She can't accept both invitations, but it might be upsetting to have to refuse one of them. I have had the honour to meet the lady in question. She is undoubtedly a woman of rare virtue and distinction. Which makes it even more important, I'm sure you agree, that her sensibilities are not put to the test of so thankless a choice.'

'You mean neither of them should ask her?'

'Not at all, A.B., not at all. One, but not both. As I see it – and I'm sure our friends would agree with me here – it is our duty as gentlemen to protect such a paragon of femininity from such a trial. And, dare I say it, our duty as members of the Asadi Club?'

'Exactly what are you suggesting, Tiger?'

'I am suggesting, A.B., that there must be a fair way of deciding who should have the honour of first invitation.'

'Right on.' Harry Khan was grinning from ear to ear. 'So what's it going to be – poker, billiards, arm-wrestling?'

'Counting hadadas?' said Patel, failing to stifle a giggle.

As a drowning man is said to clutch at a straw, from his mael-strom of embarrassment and confusion Mr Malik clutched at that word.

'Yes, that's it,' he said.

'What's it?' said Mr Gopez.

'Birds.'

'Birds?' said the Tiger.

'Oh, I see,' said Mr Gopez. 'A bit of augury you want is it, a bit of divination? Spread out the entrails and see what they say?'

'No, a contest, a competition. Counting birds. Who can identify the most species of birds in . . . in a week, say.'

'I think I see what you mean, Malik old chap,' said Mr Patel. 'If you win, you pop that invitation to the Hunt Club Ball into the postbox. If you lose, Khan over there gets to dial her number.'

'This may indeed be the solution we have been seeking,' said the Tiger. 'But *audi et alteram partem*, don't you know. We'd better find out what Khan here has to say.'

Harry Khan smiled a slow smile. Hell, this might even be more fun than Elvira.

'Maybe you'll see that red bishop this time, eh Malik? And oh, yeah, now I remember that name we used to call you. It wasn't Mack – it was Jack. Right?'

Mr Malik winced.

'OK, Jack, it's a deal. Birds it is.'

'There could be a slight problem here, Tiger,' said Mr Patel. 'One of the potential participants in this contest is not, as far as I know, a member of this club.'

'Proposed,' said Mr Malik.

'Seconded,' said A. B. Gopez in a somewhat louder voice.

'Sign him up, Mr Patel,' said the Tiger. 'Sign him up.'

Godwit

14

'May I first say, fellow club members – and with a special welcome to our newest member – what a great honour it is for me to be called upon to facilitate in the matter of Malik versus Khan.'

The Tiger, having spent the remainder of the previous night consulting with said parties and the following morning at his chambers together with Mr Patel and Mr Gopez (the three of them having volunteered to form the ad hoc committee overseeing the contest), was about to announce the 'rules of engagement' to a packed Asadi Club. He took a document from his briefcase and placed it on the table before him.

'But *a posse ad esse* – let us cut to the chase.' Removing the pink ribbon from the several sheets of paper he cleared his throat. 'It has been agreed by the two members now before us, Mr Malik and Mr Khan (hereafter known as the protagonists), that they will make a Wager. The winner of that Wager will have the privilege of asking Mrs Rose Mbikwa (hereafter known as the lady) to the Nairobi Hunt Club Ball of November the twenty-fifth coming. The losing party agrees to refrain from issuing such an invitation unless and until the lady in question gives a firm reply in the negative to the first invitation. Both parties also agree that between now and the moment when the Wager is settled, neither will initiate contact – personal, telephonic or epistolary, nor through any third person nor by any other means – with the aforementioned lady.'

The Tiger let his gaze wander over his assembled audience, then back to the document in his hand.

'The substance of the Wager is as follows,' he continued. 'That starting at noon tomorrow, Saturday October fourteenth, and finishing at noon on Saturday October twenty-first, each protagonist will make a list of all bird species he is able to identify at first hand. The protagonist able to identify the highest number of species during these seven days will be judged to have won the Wager. The result of the Wager will be decided by the ad hoc Committee of the Wager (hereafter referred to as the Committee), whose judgement will be final. The decision will be handed down as soon as possible after noon on the final day of the Wager, that is to say Saturday October twenty-first. Gentlemen, are you in agreement so far?'

A stiff nod from Mr Malik, a 'You bet' from Harry Khan; a murmur from the crowded bar.

'In that case, the details of the Wager – which shall be binding on both protagonists – are as follows.

'One: Bird species will be recognized according to the 1996 *Official Checklist of the Birds of Africa*. Subspecies are not eligible, even when described in more recent publications as full species.

'Two: Birds must be alive and uninjured at time of identification.

'Three: Birds must be in a state of nature, and in no way caged, tethered or otherwise confined.

'Four: Identification must be visual. Identification by call, tracks, scats or pellets, nests or unattached feathers is not allowable.

'Five: The use of bait, lures, tethered birds or pre-recorded sound to attract birds is strictly forbidden.

'Six: Optical aids in the form of spectacles, binoculars, telescopes and other passive devices may be used at any time. Cameras (photographic or digital), video equipment (including night vision enhancers) or electronic equipment of any other sort are strictly forbidden.

'Seven: All sightings must be within one day's travel of the Asadi Club, and within the territorial boundaries of the Republic of Kenya, including riverine, lacustrine and offshore islands.

'Eight: To help ensure compliance with the above rule, each protagonist will be required to attend the club between the hours of seven p.m. and eight p.m., and no later than eight p.m., on each of the days during which the procedure of the Wager takes place.

'Nine: At this time on each day they will be required to inform a member of the Committee of any sightings of that day, who will add them to the Master List, which will be posted, together with a copy of this agreement, on the club noticeboard.

'Ten: Both or either protagonist may appeal to the Committee during the period from seven p.m. to eight p.m. on any day during the procedure of the Wager, for rulings on either the substance of the Wager or the details of the Wager. The rulings of the Committee will be available to both of the protagonists and its judgement will be final.'

Tiger Singh looked up from the document.

'Gentlemen, are you willing to abide by these details?'

'Yes,' said Mr Malik.

'Yep,' said Harry Khan.

'I have two more things to say. Firstly . . .' and the Tiger surveyed the assembled crowd with his full magisterial authority, 'that in accordance with established etiquette this matter is not to be discussed outside the club. Remember, all of you, that a lady is involved. Secondly, the Committee wishes to attach the following observation. In a case of this sort, strict enforcement of the rules is impossible. A fair result depends absolutely on the honesty and integrity of the protagonists, both as men of honour and as members of the Asadi Club.'

Tiger Singh looked each man in the eye. For once Harry Khan was not smiling.

'*Audentes fortuna juvat*, gentlemen. May the best man win.'

All night long in his lonely bed Mr Malik was tossed about by restless waves of worry and regret. Oh foolish Malik. Oh rash and reckless Malik. What had inspired him to make such a challenge? How on earth could he hope to win? But he'd done it now, and honour demanded he try his damnedest. How many different birds were there in Kenya – more than a thousand, wasn't it? He wouldn't be able to travel far from the city – commitments were commitments. How many could you see around Nairobi – two hundred, three? Where should he go, what should he do? Why, oh why, had he written that invitation to Rose Mbikwa in the first place?

Harry Khan, after another night on the town with his obliging niece, slept well. He appeared late at the hotel breakfast room, though not too late to find a few other people still tucking into the buffet. He already had a plan. After his usual small omelette and coffee and croissant he would tootle over to the travel desk and get them to arrange a few one-day safaris. With the right guides he was sure to see plenty of birds. He deserved a holiday. Business could wait. This might be fun.

Now, if only he could remember *why* they used to call old Malik 'Jack' . . .

Great Egret

15

Among the other late breakfasters in the Hilton dining room Harry recognized David and George, whom you will remember as the Australian couple at Tuesday's bird walk whose abundance of pockets had immediately identified them as tourists. To narrow their identification still further, David and George (the one with the beard) were what are known in the travel trade as ecotourists. Not for them a luxury cruise around the Caribbean or a guided tour of the nine great medieval cities of Eastern Europe. On their holidays from their jobs in Sydney teaching the reluctant schoolchildren of Wooloomooloo High the language of Shakespeare, Dylan Thomas and Les Murray they preferred to spend their time and hard-earned money visiting Antarctica to see seals and penguins, the Galapagos Islands for tortoises and finches, or the high Andes for guanacos and condors. At the end of yet another twelve-week stretch they had come to Kenya not to laze by the warm Indian Ocean or visit the tea and coffee plantations of the hill country, but for the wildlife.

For not without reason is Kenya safari capital of the world.

If it is elephants, lions, rhinoceroses and hippos that you want to see, Kenya is the place to see them. The country is wildlife heaven and these days, thanks partly to Rose Mbikwa, there are whole hosts of people ready to help you enter its gates – hoteliers, game wardens, drivers, pilots and guides. David and George were themselves just back from a short safari to the Maasai Mara, where from a hot-air balloon they had witnessed the famed migration of a million wildebeest and zebra across the plains, and when out spotlighting at night had seen a pride of lions reduce that million by two – one of each. They hadn't originally come for the birds but after their experience at the MEATI the previous Tuesday had become quite enthusiastic. It was to this subject that the breakfast conversation turned after Harry Khan joined them and told them about his own desire to begin some serious birdwatching.

'We saw a hundred and eighty, and that was just in a few days,' said George.

'We wrote them down,' said David, buttering his third croissant. 'I was expecting the elephants and lions, but I hadn't thought there would be so many birds.'

'Mind you, our driver was pretty good at spotting them – right, Davo? Eyes like an eagle.'

'Not too good on the names, but you can always look them up in the book.'

'And we weren't even looking for them, really, were we, Davo? Wonderful. I mean, it was the same with that walk we went on the other day with you, Harry. How many birds did we see then? Must have been forty, fifty species, just in a couple of hours.'

'But it sounds like you're on a bit of a tight schedule. How long did you say you've got?'

'Seven days,' said Harry. 'Till next Saturday.'

'Hang on a tick, Davo. We're not flying back till . . .'

'You mean why don't we . . . ?'

'Great idea.'

'Could be fun, I reckon.'

'What do you say, Harry?'

Harry was finding the conversation a little hard to follow.

'I'm finding this conversation a little hard to follow, guys.'

'What Davo means is, we've got another week here,' said George.

'Yeah. We could team up.'

'Go places – find birds. Tsavo, Amboseli, maybe down to the coast. What do you say?'

Harry smiled.

'I say yes,' he said.

On the morning after the night of the bird wager we find Mr Malik in his usual place on the veranda of his house in Garden Lane, his morning Nescafé on the table before him, as Benjamin comes sweep-sweep-sweeping around the corner.

I have not yet described the effect on Benjamin of the fart – sorry, hadada – count of two days before. By the end of that day Benjamin had become quite convinced that his boss was, as they say in this part of Africa, mad as an English. What could have been viewed at the start as a mere eccentricity – if Mr Malik wanted to count hadadas or any other bird he had every right to do so – soon manifested as a symptom of some deeper malady. It had taken Benjamin no more than six minutes to realize that the only hadadas that Mr Malik was counting existed within his own head (the fact that this was accompanied by a strange tendency to fart whenever he thought he heard one was probably, thought Benjamin, only of minor concern). But anyone with that many large brown birds aroost in his cranium and that much gas in his bottom was clearly not a well person. Probably harm-less, but certainly not well. Benjamin could not help being reminded of the woman in the village where he grew up, who during an apparently normal conversation would start grasping invisible objects from the air and putting them in her apron. Perhaps he should speak to Mr Malik's daughter about it. She had always seemed a friendly and sympathetic person.

But compared to the fears and worries of Benjamin that morning, those of Mr Malik were as a toothache to a tickle. What, oh what, was he going to do? He hadn't the faintest notion. And when three hours later he looked at his watch and realized that it was time to climb into the old Mercedes and head for the club for the start of the contest, still no idea – faint or otherwise – had come to him.

For a Saturday morning the car park was unusually full. Mr Malik was surprised to see Harry Khan already at the bar – he hadn't noticed a red convertible outside. Patel and A.B. were sitting at their usual table, keeping a respectable distance from the protagonist as befitted their positions as members of the Special Committee. Clothed in weekend casuals of startling vibrance, in swept the Tiger.

If you have been to a boxing match or a cockfight you will have a good idea of the excitement buzzing through the club. When the hands of the old clock above the bar showed five minutes to twelve the Tiger stood up and called for silence. He reminded the audience of the serious yet magnificent nature of the undertaking now before these two respected members of the Asadi Club. Athens and Sparta, Rome and Carthage, David, Goliath and Winston Churchill were each called upon to give support to his case. Indeed so carried away was the Tiger by his own eloquence that he appeared not to notice the time. But no matter. Sanjay Bashu had borrowed a starting pistol from somewhere and as the minute hand reached the top of the clock, he took it from his pocket. Pointing the muzzle ceilingward, he pulled the trigger. Nothing happened, but the resulting cheer was the signal for Harry Khan to give a wide wave to the assembled crowd and head for the car park where a Nissan safari bus was now revving its engine, driver at the wheel. George and David pulled Harry into the vehicle and slammed shut the door. With a screech of tyres and to the cheers of the crowd now assembled on the front steps of the club, the bus took off towards whichever secret Mecca of birdlife had been chosen for that afternoon's birdspotting. It was at that moment that Sanjay Bashu discovered the safety catch on the starting pistol and again pulled the trigger. The bang of the pistol echoed off the walls of the Asadi Club like the report of an elephant gun, followed by a cacophony of flaps and screeches from a tall maru tree in the corner of the car park.

'Hadadas,' yelled out Mr Patel, dissolving into such a fit of giggles that he had to be helped back up the steps by A. B. Gopez and into the bar.

Pied Crow

16

Sitting on his veranda that afternoon back at Number 12 Garden Lane, Mr Malik turned to a fresh page of his notebook. He paused, listened and looked up into the croton trees at the end of the garden.

'Day 1,' he wrote. And underneath, 'Hadada.'

He should never have told the chaps at the club about the hadada thing – especially Patel. With a sigh he put down the pad and pencil. So many things he should never have done. He should never have issued the challenge, he should never have told them about Rose Mbikwa, he should never have written her that invitation. His sigh became a groan. He should never have been born.

A pied crow hopped noisily across the roof and glided down on to the lawn, landing with its customary caw and shuffle of wings. He stared at it for several seconds, then picked up the pad and pencil once more. From the bougainvillea opposite a pair of mousebirds emerged, fluttered across to an ornamental fig and began chasing each other among the branches, looking not like mice exactly but distinctly un-birdlike. But you could see a mousebird more or less anywhere. Who knows what ornithological wonders were being recorded by Harry Khan, wherever he was? Eagles, ostriches, secretary birds? Mr Malik wrote down 'Pied crow' and 'Speckled mousebird' and got to his feet. If he was going to sit here all afternoon, he supposed he may as well get his binoculars. Who knows, he might spot a sparrow.

Harry Khan had not in fact seen a secretary bird, an eagle, nor even an ostrich. At the very moment that Mr Malik was going into his house at Number 12 Garden Lane to fetch his Bausch & Lombs, Harry Khan was sitting in the front of the Nissan safari bus just past the football stadium on the Limuru Road in a traffic jam. In the excitement of the morning he had failed to tune into 2KJ for the traffic report, and therefore failed to learn that the President was arriving back that very afternoon from his overseas trip. Roads were closed, traffic was being diverted; the result was gridlock. Even the matatus, those overcrowded minibuses whose drivers' ability to move through traffic is generally accepted to owe more to witchcraft than the laws of physics, were immobile.

In the Nissan, George and David were trying to make the best of it. They had already pointed out to Harry several crows and pigeons, and thought that they'd seen a marabou stork flying high overhead but couldn't be absolutely sure. After an hour of going nowhere Harry decided he'd had enough birdwatching for one day. They were not yet too far out of town for him to walk back to the Hilton – he could still see the tall hotel on the skyline behind them. At that moment a shower and a cool drink were more important than an early lead. Leaving a sweating driver and a still optimistic David and George – 'It's bound to sort itself out soon, Harry – right, Davo?' – to fend for themselves, he set off on foot back to the hotel.

Night falls quickly in Nairobi. Only one degree south of the equator, at six o'clock it is full daylight, at six thirty pitch black.

Mr Malik arrived at the club just as the outside lights were turned on, which is to say at six fifteen on the dot. In his hand was the notebook containing the birds he had seen that afternoon, the whole of which he had spent in his garden. Patel began transcribing their names on to a piece of foolscap paper. 'Hadada (stifled giggle), pied crow, mousebird . . .' The Tiger arrived soon after, followed shortly by Harry Khan, looking relaxed and refreshed. Though his walk back to the hotel had not been pleasant (walking anywhere in the city seldom is), he had managed to fit in a shower, a swim, a snooze and a drink before driving over to the club. He too passed a notebook to Patel, who looked at it with some surprise but said nothing. At ten to seven the Tiger called for hush in the bar.

'Firstly, gentlemen, may I say how pleased we are to see you both here – *dimidium facti qui coepit habet* and all that. And I must ask you, according to the rules of the competition, whether there are any points that either of you wishes to raise with the Committee.'

Mr Malik shook his head and turned towards the newest member.

'Yes,' said Harry Khan. 'Would any of you care to join me for a beer?'

There was much laughter and several other members volunteered to join the Special Committee then and there.

'Mr Patel,' called out the Tiger. 'Do you have the results for the first day?'

Patel held up a hand while he checked through each list.

'I have,' he said. 'Malik, thirty-one. Khan . . . three.'

There was a stunned silence.

'Did you say three, Mr Patel?'

Patel read from the list. 'Crow, pigeon, kite – that is all, though there is no indication of what kind of crow, pigeon and kite and I seem to remember that according to the checklist there are several of each.'

'No doubt those would be pied crow, feral pigeon and black kite,' murmured Mr Malik to the Tiger, who nodded.

Harry Khan began a rueful explanation of how he had planned to spend the afternoon in Nairobi National Park but got caught up in the traffic, and even made his failure to check up on the movements of 'El Presidente' and his forced walk back to the hotel sound quite amusing. So everyone felt very sorry for him and ended up buying him drinks instead of the other way round. Mr Malik went to sit down at his usual table.

'Shame about poor old Khan,' said Patel, 'but you didn't do too badly, Malik. Not badly at all. Keep that up and you'll be in with a chance – wouldn't you say, A.B.?'

'Won't happen,' said Mr Gopez. 'Stands to reason. You're bound to see all the common ones early on, then new ones'll get scarcer and scarcer. Law of diminishing returns.'

'Is that right, Malik?' said Patel. 'What do you say?'

Mr Malik had in fact been giving this matter, and others, much thought. The afternoon's tally had surprised him. He'd sat in the garden before, of course, and he'd noticed birds there, but never so many. Why was this, he wondered? He had seen birds that afternoon that he had never seen in the garden before – a common drongo perched on the telephone wire for instance, and a grey woodpecker flying from tree to tree. Not all of the birds stopped in the garden, of course, but it was amazing how many had flown over close enough to be identified – black kites and needle-tailed swifts and red-rumped swallows – even a pied cormorant flying high but quite recognizable, on its way from goodness knows where to goodness knows where else. Thirty-one different species, about five an hour – not bad for an afternoon's work. At that rate if he just sat in the garden all day for the next week he would see almost half the country's avifauna. But there was a simple flaw in this argument, and Mr Malik had spotted it long before A. B. Gopez. In one afternoon he may well have seen most of the local birds he was ever likely to see. If he wanted to capitalize on his early lead, he would have to go further afield than the walls and hedges of Number 12 Garden Lane. Which, given the nature of his commitments, would not be easy.

'Commitments?' I hear you say. 'What commitments?' Have I not already let it be known that Mr Malik is now in semi-retirement? Have I not explained that most of the day-to-day running of the Jolly Man Manufacturing Company is now under-taken by Mr Malik's able but still-single daughter Petula? So what commitments are these that could prevent Mr Malik spending each and all of the six and a half days remaining out and about, here and there, up hill and down dale, in pursuit of as many different species of Kenyan birds as he could find and hence into the arms of the woman of his dreams in the ballroom of the Suffolk Hotel? Well, there is charity work – that takes up a surprising amount of time. But there is something else, some-thing that Mr Malik has been doing every Tuesday afternoon after the bird walk for the last two and a half years. There is nothing else for it.

I will now have to reveal another of Mr Malik's secrets.

Black Eagle

17

Think back to your first visit to the Asadi Club. You will remember that as Mr Malik enters, Mr Patel and A. B. Gopez are seated at their usual table. Mr Gopez is reading the *Evening News* and becoming more apoplectic by the moment. We discover that what is raising his blood pressure is not the leader, not the latest news from Buckingham Palace nor something in 'Birds of a Feather' but a small story about Danish research into – well, you remember the rest.

But wait, what exactly is this 'Birds of a Feather'? It is a weekly column, apparently about the birds and beasts of Kenya, that appears every Wednesday on page seven of the *Nairobi Evening News*. It is not really a nature column, though. It is about politics – or to be more exact, politicians.

If you want the inside information on what the elected members are up to, the stories behind the stories, the good oil, this is where you find them. It is where the scandals break, the deals are revealed, the curtains (and sometimes sheets) are lifted. In the tradition of such pieces, the byline is a pen-name – in this case 'Dadukwa', which those with a knowledge of African mythology will recognize as the name of the black eagle who, seeing all but never seen, spreads the news among the other animals. No one knows the identity of the brave journalist (or politician, or civil servant perhaps?) who shelters behind this pseudonym. The copy, hand typed and anonymous, is delivered to the offices of the *Nairobi Evening News* every Wednesday morning by first post. It has been arriving every Wednesday for the last two and a half years, and is the reason that an extra fifteen thousand copies of the *News* are printed that day, for that is how popular it has become.

But surely a responsible newspaper editor should know the identity of all the writers he publishes? What happened was this. Nearly three years ago the editor of the *Evening News* received in the mail a short typed note.

'You have no natural history column,' it said. 'Would you like me to write you one?'

The note was signed with an illegible scrawl above a typed name, Mr Dadukwa. The address was a post office box at Nairobi GPO. The editor thought for a bit then dictated a reply to his secretary to the effect that although a column of this sort might be suitable for the *Evening News* he regretted that – what with union rules, publisher's regulations and printing overheads – no payment was possible for such material. The following Wednesday's mail contained another typewritten letter, together with a short piece about the birds that might be seen in and around the National Arboretum. It was headed 'Birds of a Feather'. The piece seemed innocuous and well enough written. The editor passed it over to the chief sub and thought no more about it.

The column was published and the next week the editor received a description of the elephants that used to be found in Nairobi National Park and he printed that too. And so it went. Every Wednesday morning the copy would arrive in the mail – about elephants or baboons or vultures or whatever it was

– and the editor would glance at it, pass it to the chief sub and it would be printed in that afternoon's paper. This is after all what every editor dreams of, regular free copy. Some day he would perhaps meet this Mr Dadukwa, but he was in no hurry to do so.

A couple of months later he was leaving the Thursday morning editorial meeting.

'Great column yesterday, boss,' said one of his reporters.

In a hurry to meet a new friend in town he just said, 'Yeah, good,' so it wasn't until he was lying in bed later that morning with his new friend smoking a well-earned cigarette that it occurred to him that the only regular column that appears on Wednesday (a notoriously slow news day whether in Nairobi or New York) was the 'Birds of a Feather' column.

'Do you ever read the nature column?' he said to his new friend.

She said she didn't, but she had a copy of Wednesday's paper. Together they turned to page seven to read a piece about jackals and hyenas fighting over the body of a dead gazelle while the lion, who had killed the gazelle, looked on with apparent indifference. A vulture appeared. That was all. 'Eeugh,' said his new friend. The editor put on his trousers and went back to the office.

A couple of weeks later he caught two of his junior advertising managers laughing over another piece on page seven of the Wednesday paper.

'Near the bone, that one, boss,' said one of them.

He snatched the paper from them and read in 'Birds of a Feather' a story about a hippopotamus and a marabou stork.

'Will someone tell me what's going on here?'

It was left to his parliamentary reporter and letters editor to explain that the 'Birds of a Feather' column was not all it seemed. Though it could be read as a slightly idiosyncratic nature column, it was in fact a spoof, a satire. The lion, who else could that be but the President? The hippopotamus, it was obvious from appearance alone, must be the Minister of Agriculture and Tourism. The marabou was the Minister of Defence; the python, the Secretary of State for External Affairs; the hyena, Minister of the Armed Forces; the aardvark, his vociferous and deeply unpopular wife. The herds of gazelle, zebra, wildebeest etc. could each be identified with a tribal grouping or alliance, and so it went. And had he looked recently at those graphs of sales figures that appeared on his desk each week? The upward blip on Wednesday could mean only one thing. The column was popular.

The editor thought he had better find out who was writing this stuff. At first he suspected it might be one of his own staff. At the next morning's editorial meeting he began by referring to the brilliance of the column – he had wondered how long the others would take to spot the joke – but now it was time for its writer to reveal himself, and to collect his reward. No one stood up, no one spoke.

'Come on now, gentlemen. It must be one of you, and it's only fair to pay you for your fine work.'

Everyone looked around at all the other people in the room, but still no one spoke.

'I quite understand,' said the editor, and he did. Though Kenya has a free press its democratic government, like many governments both democratic and not, has not always seen this as an advantage. As the editor (and Rose Mbikwa) well knew, there are many ways to silence criticism and to a person who decides to speak out prudent anonymity may well be preferable to a few extra shillings in the pay packet. In Kenya, people still disappear. But could it be that the writer was indeed not present? The editor found the original letter from Mr Dadukwa, dated 16th February (his chief political reporter, an Akamba man, had already explained the significance of the pseudonym). A junior reporter was despatched to find the owner of the post office box and discovered that a Mr J. Aripo had been renting it since April. He was sent back with the clear conviction that if he did not find out who had been renting the post office box on 16th February he could say *kwaheri* to his career in journalism. Three hours and several hundred persuasive shillings later he returned to the newspaper office with the news that the box had indeed been rented at that time to a Mr Dadukwa, who as far as the clerk could remember was a youngish or possibly middle-aged man of African or Asian appearance, dressed in darkish clothing but definitely with no noticeable deformity or speech impediment.

Which meant very little to the editor, but which you will no doubt recognize as an uncannily accurate description of . . . Mr Malik.

Oriole

18

There is a distressing but not uncommon condition of presidents and other world leaders known as Worrying about Africa. It is usually picked up overseas at a summit meeting on world poverty or disease, and symptoms include painful twinges of guilt over the discrepancy between First and Third World wealth, uncomfortable feelings somewhere below the stomach that perhaps unfettered capitalism is not the benevolent force for good we are constantly assured it is, and frequent attacks of calling for Something to Be Done. The best remedy is invariably a stiff dose of domestic crisis.

During the early part of his second term President Clinton went through a short but intense attack of the condition, and before young Monica arrived to administer the cure he had not only set up a Special Senate Committee on Africa but sent his trusted friend and aide Dr Ronald K. Dick on a comprehensive five-day fact-finding mission to the continent. Dr Dick's extensive itinerary included nearly nine full hours in Kenya.

After hearing his report back in Washington, the Special Senate

Committee agreed that while more financial aid to the region was undoubtedly called for, this must be linked to the various efficiency measures recommended by Dr Dick (though, of course, only if freely agreed to by the governments concerned). High on the list of these measures for Kenya was a restructure of the ministerial transport arrangements. During his brief but in-depth visit to the country Dr Dick had been provided by the US embassy in Nairobi with a car and driver from the embassy car pool. Ministers in the Kenyan government, he noted, each had their own personal car and driver. This car and driver might be idle for most of the day – while the minister was in parliament or his departmental office, or having lunch or wherever else he chose to spend his time. It would clearly be more efficient if car and driver could be used elsewhere during these periods of idleness, and the way to ensure this would be a car pool – why, just like the one they have at the good old US embassy. The senators were so impressed with this simple but effective recommendation that they made it one of their key conditions for further aid to Kenya. No car pool, no cash. The sovereign government of the Republic of Kenya freely agreed to this condition. Among the people affected by their decision was Thomas Nyambe, whom you have previously encountered as Mr Malik's companion on the bird walk.

Thomas Nyambe had until then been personal driver to the Minister of Education. At six o'clock every morning except Sunday he would arrive by matatu at the minister's home. He would wash the car and take the children to school (yes, even on a Saturday most children in Nairobi go to school). For the rest of the day he would be on call for the minister – sometimes taking him to his office, or to parliament, or wherever else the minister's work and whim demanded. Now his work schedule changed. In any one day he might find himself taking the Minister of Tourism to the airport for an early flight, the Minister of Agriculture to a restaurant for a luncheon appointment, and the wife of the Secretary of State for Trade to the market in the afternoon (for as the

Minister of Transport explained to the senior under-secretary at the US embassy in charge of car-pool compliance, it was surely more efficient using a government car to drive wives and family around rather than the ministers having to do it themselves). And he now got Sundays and rostered Tuesday mornings off.

Thomas Nyambe had always been a government driver. He was the son of a government driver. When his father's eyes got so bad that, squint though he might, he was unable to drive into the sun without being completely blinded, he had passed on his job and his uniform to Thomas. His father taught Thomas how to drive, and how to be a driver. So Thomas learned not only how to operate and look after a vehicle, but how to play the part that employers expect their drivers to play – safe and silent.

Ask any taxi driver and they will tell you that they sometimes get the feeling that they are invisible. People in the back of a taxi will talk about their most important and intimate affairs as if there was no one else there, as if the car was driving itself. It is the same with government drivers. Though Thomas's father had told him all about this, he had not taught him how to read and write and neither had anyone else. Thomas Nyambe could 'read' road signs, of course (though this skill is seldom called for in Kenya, the paint on the few road signs that exist being usually faded to illegibility). He knew all about numbers and money. He knew to the nearest shilling the cost of petrol, oil (both engine and transmission), how much it costs to fix a little puncture, a big puncture, and all the other things that a government driver needs to know. But the world of letters hardly entered his consciousness, and though he learned much about the workings of government and the doings of the government ministers while driving his car, and from talking to other drivers in the car pool, it wouldn't have occurred to him to record any of this information any more than it would have to record the birds he saw on the Tuesday morning bird walks which he had regularly attended on his rostered morning off for the last five years.

★　★　★

Mr Malik had first met Thomas Nyambe outside the Nairobi Museum on his very first Tuesday morning bird walk. Despite a warm welcome from Rose Mbikwa, Mr Malik had been feeling a little awkward, a little out of place. A black man whom he had noticed standing back from the others, always smiling but never speaking, came over and introduced himself, and from that moment on he and Thomas Nyambe became friends. It really was just like that. It's happened to me, and it's probably happened to you. From the first exchange of good mornings they had recognized in each other a kindred soul. Though neither spoke much to start with, they felt an immediate ease in each other's company that was both surprising and yet the most natural thing in the world.

As they exchanged more and more words over the following weeks Thomas Nyambe found out that Mr Malik was a widower and Mr Malik found out that Thomas Nyambe had worked for the government as a government driver for nearly thirty years. He had a wife called Hyacinth and seven children, two of whom had recently died.

'I too have a son who is dead,' said Mr Malik. Even now, after four years, he seldom talked about his son.

Mr Nyambe told Mr Malik that he lived in Southlands, but over the years he and his brother had saved up enough money to buy a small farm on the coast just north of Malindi, where their father had come from. His brother was building a house there now and would then build another for him and that is where they would move to when he retired from his job as a government driver.

'It is good to have your own land and grow your own food. And you, Mr Malik, will you ever move out of Nairobi?'

'I am no farmer, Mr Nyambe. My grandfather used to grow vegetables, but I think I must take after my father. It is said that the soil in Nairobi is so rich that if you planted a seed you must stand back quickly – so as not to be injured by the growing plant, you know. My father could have planted a thousand seeds and the only injury he risked was cutting his foot on the hoe. He was not a farmer, and neither am I. I think I will stay in Nairobi.'

'But there are more birds to be seen on a farm than in the city, is this not so?'

'This is true, Mr Nyambe, and as you know I like watching birds. But I see them in my garden and around town and as long as I keep coming on the Tuesday bird walks I will keep seeing them.'

Yet behind his mild exterior Mr Malik's new friend was a passionate man. His passions were his family, his birds and his country.

Guineafowl

19

Like Mr Malik, Thomas Nyambe had grown up in a Nairobi very different from today's sprawling city. Back then, the city centre was just a few streets surrounded by parks and gardens. The river was lined not with the cardboard shacks of the slum-dwellers but with papyrus. On the short walk from the GPO to the railway station you might see a family of guineafowl running across the road, or a night-heron roosting in its favourite fever tree in the Governor General's garden.

'There are still some birds to be seen, as you know, Mr Malik. But now you have to go a long way to see a night-heron, or even a guineafowl.'

For Mr Nyambe, to be able to go and watch birds with like-minded people in comfortable cars, that was indeed a joy and a privilege. There is something about birds, their beauty and freedom, that is good for a man's soul. But a man who is saving money to buy a farm and build a house cannot afford to fritter away his shillings on buses or matatus just to get out of town for the morning, even if it is for his soul. On bird walk days Mr

Nyambe invariably travelled in the front passenger seat of Mr Malik's old green Mercedes. Of course, he always made sure that he brought along a little something – some spiced pea-cakes or sugar biscuits that his wife Hyacinth made for him to take – to show his appreciation to whoever might give him a lift. Mr Malik had grown to quite like pea-cake, though he would only eat one sugar biscuit and that was out of politeness.

Mr Nyambe's love for Kenya was as strong as his love for birds.

'There is surely no other country like it, Mr Malik. Where else can you find a snow-capped mountain of such magnificence as our own Mount Kenya, and a coast of palm-lined beaches? What other country has deserts and forests, lakes and rivers, hills and plains like ours? Where else are the men so handsome and the women so beautiful?'

'And where else, Mr Nyambe, can you see so many birds?'

'Not only birds, Mr Malik. Lions, elephants.'

'Cheetahs, giraffes.'

'Impala.'

'Gazelle.'

'Warthogs.'

'Bush pigs.'

'Wildebeest.'

'Hartebeest.'

'It is true, Mr Malik. We are blessed. It is a fine country that we live in.'

As the friendship between the two men grew, Mr Nyambe found himself talking more freely about his work, which was something he seldom did, even to his wife.

'That marabou,' he said, pointing to a bird that stood tall and funereal beside a rubbish heap as they strolled together down Two Rivers Road on the bird walk one day. 'It is not a pretty bird, Mr Malik. I am sure you have seen them, always fighting with the other birds – the crows and the egrets. Marabou is the nickname we – the drivers in the car pool, you know – give to the Minister of Defence. He is not a good man. He says he is a Christian, but do you know how many wives he has?'

Mr Malik raised a quizzical eyebrow.

'More than the usual number?'

'Three – one in Kisumu, one in Kakamega and one in Nairobi. That is too many for one Christian man.'

'That is too many for any man, Mr Nyambe.'

'I think you are right, Mr Malik.'

Mr Nyambe gave a sudden grin.

'But the water snake – I mean Mr Matiba, the Minister for Security, you know – he thinks the Nairobi wife is his wife, so perhaps that makes it only two.'

And so it went. Each Tuesday Mr Malik would offer Mr Nyambe a lift in his old green Mercedes and the two men would talk about birds and politics. Why is it that the little purple-banded sunbird likes to build its nests on the verandas of men, and does the female grey hornbill mind being sealed up by the male in a hollow tree behind a mud wall while she sits on her eggs? If the Minister for Education needs a new house, should he not buy the land to build it on rather than being deeded two acres of Karura State Forest by the Minister for Forests and Fisheries – for are not the State Forests for everybody? – and just why does the Secretary of the Treasury need to take so many private flights to Switzerland?

'There is much thoughtlessness in the world, Mr Malik. Though I do not see it among ordinary people, among rich people and powerful people it is common. But when the elephant reaches for the plantains he does not see the shamba fence. It is us who elect them, is it not? Perhaps it is up to us to make them see what they are doing.'

His friend's words stayed with Mr Malik. It did not happen immediately, but after a few weeks a dim light began to glow in his brain. Yes, somebody should indeed make these men see what they were doing. It was all very well to vote every few years, but was that enough? It was all very well to complain, but what did that achieve? Someone should do something. It took nearly two months for Mr Malik to work out that that someone was him. He was the one who must do it. Had he not longed to be a journalist in those far-off London days? Was this not the very opportunity he had been looking for, the chance to make a difference? That very morning he went into the city and rented a post office box. That afternoon he wrote a letter to the editor of the *Evening News*.

And the next Tuesday after the bird walk he typed his very first 'Birds of a Feather' column on to a sheet of plain white A4 paper, sealed it in an envelope and popped it into the postbox at the corner of Garden Lane and Parklands Drive.

Purple Backed Sunbird

20

The ostrich was growing used to this. Each day just after dawn the monstrous beast behind the fence would awake and begin to roar. Slowly it turned towards him, slowly it advanced, its bellowing growing louder, its strange eyes reflecting the orange of the rising sun. The ostrich was a male and had a nest to protect. The shallow pit he had dug unaided with his bare claws now contained sixteen eggs that had been laid there by the three females he had courted and mated with. The eggs were only days from hatching. The ostrich drew himself up to his full three-metre height, fluffed out his wings to make him look as big as he could, and began to strut, stiff-legged and unblinking, in the direction of the fence. Onwards came the monster, straight towards him. Closer they approached each other and closer still. The beast's roar was like a lion and a buffalo and an elephant all rolled into one, but the ostrich neither flinched nor faltered. It was the beast which turned. It turned on to the long track that led away from the fence and with a last roar sped down the track and off into the rising sun.

The ostrich fluffed its feathers once more, folded them, and returned to the nest. The monster would be back, he was sure of it, but he would be ready.

As the early flight to Lamu turned at the bottom of the runway at Wilson Aerodrome ready for take-off, Harry Khan looked out of the window.

'Hey, guys, look – an ostrich, there, just behind the fence. First bird of the day – got to be a good sign.'

Harry Khan had spent the previous night at the bar of the Hilton with George and David planning the week's itinerary.

'The first thing we should do,' said George, 'is get the weather forecast. Right, Davo? It's no good going to the hills if they're covered in fog, and it's no good going to the coast if there's a hurricane blowing.'

With David's laptop tuned into the hotel's wireless internet system they established that there was a nasty-looking low just off Madagascar and indeed a high possibility of strong winds on the coast early next week.

'Better get down there asap,' said David.

'Yep,' said George, 'tick off the shore and seabirds first, then do the inland stuff.'

'Makes sense to me,' said Harry.

From their Lonely Planet guidebook they discovered that the island of Lamu would probably be their best bet for a day trip. A flight left at dawn and the mid-afternoon flight back to Nairobi would give them plenty of time to get to the Asadi Club by eight o'clock.

'It says here you can hire a boat to explore the island and the numerous nearby lagoons.'

'Sounds like just the spot,' said Harry and went over to the hotel travel desk to book the tickets. This should be fun. Shame about the early start.

Unlike the ostrich, the yellow-crested woodpecker was showing no signs of alarm at the monstrous figure approaching. Born and bred in City Park, it had grown used to two-legged creatures like the one now walking towards its tree. These things, large as they were, were not half as much trouble as the monkeys – though this one did have rather large eyes. The woodpecker continued to peck wood; Mr Malik lowered his binoculars to record in his notebook the first new bird of the day.

His surprise at the number of species that he had seen in his garden the previous afternoon had given Mr Malik an idea. Of course, what A.B. had said about diminishing returns was quite right. But, he reasoned, returns could also be diminished by spending time that might be spent birdwatching in travelling. Driving or flying here and there used up too much time in simply getting to places – especially when a condition of the competition was that both parties had to be back in Nairobi by eight o'clock every night, and even if he had had no other commitments. He therefore devised a strategy of minimum travel. Taking his house in Garden Lane as the centre he would move outwards in a rough spiral, over the week reaching more and more distant habitats. Though there were bound to be overlaps between each place he visited, this plan should optimize his chance of seeing the most species. He chose for his first visit City Park, only a mile or two from his house and a place he knew well.

Like much of Nairobi, City Park has seen better days. Compared with the once handsome pleasure gardens of yester-year with palm-lined avenues and well-tended shrubbery, where fountains splashed and the music of Sousa and Elgar wafted from the bandstand each Sunday afternoon from three to five, the park is down on its luck. But the park still gives pleasure to those of the city's inhabitants who know of its existence, as well as giving food and shelter to numbers of squirrels and monkeys and even greater numbers of birds.

If you want to identify birds the best time is usually dawn because that is when they are at their most vocal. According to modern Western ornithology they are singing to establish or maintain territories, attract mates, reinforce species recognition and social dominance patterns, or communicate feeding opportunities. According to local African tradition, they are singing to greet the sun. Listening to the screeches of orange-bellied and red-fronted parrots, the twitters of varied, purple-backed and crescent-billed sunbirds, the trills of canary finches and the warbles of olive thrushes, Mr Malik thought that probably these two explanations were both right. He had arrived at the main entrance to the park just as the gates were being unlocked and, looking and listening, began to wander down the path. At the fountain, dry these many years and now full of leaves and litter, he found his footsteps turning towards the row of pine trees that marked the edge of the old cemetery.

Few people know about the old cemetery, screened off by the pine trees and a low wall. Behind it, tumbled stones mark the graves of the very first white settlers to Kenya – men and their memsahibs, and a disproportionate number of children who had fallen from horses or contracted malaria down at the coast and come to Nairobi for failed attempts at cures and convalescence. In the centre of the graveyard is a disused and now boarded-up chapel made of stone, and at the far end a caretaker's cottage. Though rundown, the cottage is still occupied, and as Mr Malik approached the sound of a baby crying and a crow from one of the domestic fowl that pecked around the yard gave welcome life to this place of death. This was by no means the first time Mr Malik had been to the old cemetery. It was here that he had come on a wet Saturday morning in February nearly four years ago to scatter the ashes of his only son Raj.

And he had come here so many Saturday mornings since to think about his son and to think about his sorrow, and his shame.

Puffback

21

I have told you that Mr Malik does not talk much about his son
Raj. I have not told you why. Raj was not a child when he died,
and he did not die by falling from a horse or from a fever
contracted among the mosquito-infested mangroves of the coast.
He was thirty-three years old, and he died from AIDS. And as
he lay dying, Mr Malik was feeling not love and compassion for
his son, but shame and disgust.

It had been some three years since his beautiful boy had told
his father he was gay. And what had Mr Malik said when his
brave and beautiful son, who he and his wife had always known
was a little different from other boys, told him this? He told Raj
to go, to leave, to disappear, to never darken his doors again.
What kind of son was this, he thundered, what kind of man
was this, who could admit to so unnatural, so perverted, so
shameful a practice? Go, said Mr Malik in all his righteousness,
you are not my son, my blood is not your blood, my name is
not your name. You have brought shame on your family and
disgrace to your mother's memory. And he meant every word.

Raj went away, but inside Mr Malik the rage and horror continued to burn. Oh, how sorry for himself he felt. What had he done to deserve this? Had he not already lost his wife? Now his son was lost to him, he told himself, and sons from his son. How could he hand on the business, as his father and grandfather had done before him? And he had lost face in the community, for Mr Malik was sure that although they said nothing, people knew.

Perhaps Raj already had AIDS when he told his father that he was gay, perhaps he caught it sometime later. The next thing Mr Malik heard was that Raj was dead. And what happened then to all the anger and shame and self-pity that burned so fierce within him? They vanished like a candle flame in a puff of air. Mr Malik awoke to the dark realization of what he had done and the terrible knowledge that there was absolutely nothing he could do. His son was dead. What mattered it now whether Raj was homosexual or heterosexual, whether he loved men or women? It was too late. Too late to retract those words, too late to say come home, too late to ask forgiveness from those beautiful cold lips. He knew in sudden certainty that his wife would never have done so unloving a thing. So the shame that now made it difficult for Mr Malik to talk about Raj was not shame at his son but shame at himself. And the sorrow was not at his own loss, but at the losses he had made his son endure.

It had been on that wet February day four days after the funeral, while scattering Raj's ashes at the old cemetery, that Mr Malik had looked around at the graves and headstones and realized that though there was nothing he could do for his son there was something else he could do. How many young men and women were dying at that very moment, alone and rejected? The answer, he soon found, was more than he could have imagined.

If it were influenza or smallpox that was carrying off people by the million, or even bubonic plague, perhaps people could have talked about it. But at that time in Kenya, AIDS was not talked about in polite society. This was mainly because of its association with homosexuality. In Kenya, as Mr Malik knew only too well, no one's son or daughter is gay. But what is talked about is different from what is. A disease does not discriminate. Mr Malik found the place where his son had died, a long dark room at the back of the Aga Khan Hospital, full of rows of skeletal young men and women – gay, straight, single, married – lying on beds, on mattresses on the floor or just on bare floors. Perhaps one of them was someone that Raj had once loved and been loved by. Here care was minimal, visitors few. It did not take him much longer to discover that there was at least one such room in every hospital in Nairobi.

Few of the dying even knew the name of the short, round, balding brown man who would come to sit beside them and smile and take their hand, or stroke their forehead and murmur sympathetic words. But even fewer would say that they did not feel better for his presence, and they would continue to feel just a little more at peace even after he had gone. And so the love he had denied his own son Raj found its way to many a forgotten son and daughter, though for Mr Malik it was never enough and never could be.

But today he was not here to reminisce, he was here to see birds. Mr Malik left the cemetery and wandered back into the park. He sat down on a concrete bench beside the fountain, and within twenty minutes he had seen seventeen new species. Among them were a black-backed puffback, a red-cheeked cordon-bleu (looking very dashing in its plumage of lapis lazuli) and a small flock of cut-throats. Why, he mused, looking at the mixed group of male and females, should the species be so named if only the males had the splash of crimson across the throat? But then many birds were named after only one of the sexes and it was usually the male. It was the same for the cordon-bleu (for only the male has a red cheek) and a score of others. Among birds at least, the males do seem to be the fancier dressers. More enthusiastic singers too. He heard, then saw a small dark bird perched on a tall bamboo. Against the bright sky it looked jet black rather than dark blue but there was no mistaking those red legs. It was an indigo bird, and he knew that it must be a male for the female has completely different plumage, more like that of a female sparrow. An unusual whistle attracted his attention. Could that be the distinctive two-note call of a black-fronted bush-shrike? He'd never heard one of those in the city before.

The call seemed to be coming from a low tree a short way down that overgrown path. Getting to his feet he made his way towards the sound. He had only gone a few steps down the path and had not yet spotted the source of the whistle when he noticed someone coming in the other direction. How annoying – the bird might be disturbed and fly off before he could identify it. And the path was really much too narrow to pass each other. Oh well, he hadn't gone far, he would just have to turn around, let the person out and hope for the best. Mr Malik turned, only to find that someone else had just walked on to the path behind him – two people in fact. They appeared to be young men.

It was best, he decided, not to make a fuss. The robbers might not hurt him, not unless he struggled or shouted. Without a word, Mr Malik reached into his pocket and handed over his wallet. Without a word, one of the young men took it.

'And those.'

He was pointing to the binoculars around Mr Malik's neck. Mr Malik sighed, and as he pulled the strap over his head felt the notebook being snatched from his hand. It was all he had to show what species he'd seen that morning and he couldn't expect the Committee, let alone Harry Khan, to accept his memories of what he'd seen. And these species – seventeen of them – they might make all the difference.

'I'm sure that book won't be of interest to you,' he said, reaching for it.

The young man replied with a tight smile, handing the note-book to his accomplice.

'Perhaps, *Bwana*' – his mouth softened as he spoke the word though his eyes did not – 'we will judge that. Now, what else is in your pockets?'

Mr Malik pulled out a pen and a handkerchief, trying not to rattle his key ring. It would be such a nuisance if they took the car key and he had to get a locksmith out.

'Did I hear something?' said the youth now holding the notebook. 'Did you hear something, brother?'

'I think I heard a jingle-jangle.'

Mr Malik put his hand back in his trouser pocket and pulled out the key ring.

'Here. Now, can I have my notebook back please? It's just a list of birds, that's all. You can look at it if you want.'

The young man looked carefully at the black eagle sketched on to the cover, then opened the notebook and inspected its contents, turning it upside down and back again.

'Birds you say? Why you want a list of birds?'

'It's a . . . it's my hobby. I like to look at birds. With those.'

He pointed to the binoculars.

The man looked at the notebook that was in one hand, and the key ring that was still in the other.

'How bad you want this? How bad you want it back?'

'I'd just like it. It's not valuable, I'd just like it back.'

'Suppose we make a deal, then, old man.'

'What do you mean?'

The man dangled the keys in front of Mr Malik.

'Suppose you show me where your car is right now. You show me where your car is, I give you back your book.'

This was ridiculous. If he showed them where his car was they would steal it. Without his help it was just possible that they wouldn't – as soon as they got away from this secluded path they would surely know he could call a policeman or an askari. Did they really imagine he would accept their ridiculous offer? Did they really imagine that he thought his notebook was worth more than his car? Mr Malik looked up at the robber, the key ring still dangling from the fingers of one hand, the notebook in the other.

'All right,' he said.

The old green Mercedes was parked across from the main gate. The four of them left the City Park, crossed the road, and Mr Malik watched while the three robbers opened the car, got inside and started the engine.

'My notebook, please.'

And he watched his old green Mercedes take off towards the city, the three robbers laughing away like hyenas, one of them still waving his notebook from a wound-down window.

Turtle Dove

22

'I say,' said Mr Patel when Mr Malik arrived that evening at the club, 'was that a taxi I saw you arrive in?'

Mr Malik had indeed taken a taxi to the club from the police station in Haare Thuku Road where he had spent a good part of his day. It had taken him half an hour to walk there and three hours to report the theft. He had little expectation that anything would be done – if there were no fine to be levied the police these days seemed to take little interest in criminal activity – but it was what a good citizen should do. He had then gone home to get his passport (a forty-minute walk – the police offered to let him make a phone call to his family but he didn't want to bother Petula), then taken a taxi to his bank to report that his wallet and various cards had been stolen (a speedy two and a half hours). He then had to go back to the police station so that they could fill in on their forms the numbers on the cards that had been stolen (only two hours this time). There had been no time to go back home before he was due at the club.

Mr Malik ordered a beer and gave a brief account of the doings of his day.

'What I can't see is why he went to the police,' said Mr Gopez. 'Damned robbers were probably off-duty constabulary.'

'Ah well, it's over now,' said Mr Patel. 'So, where's the jolly notebook?'

'They took that too,' said Mr Malik.

'But what about the birds?' said Mr Patel.

'Birds?' said Mr Gopez. 'Can't you think about anything else? Poor chap's been robbed blind, practically cleaned out – cash, cards and car – and all you can think about is birds?'

'Sorry A.B., I didn't mean to be . . . well, whatever I was being. Notebook stolen, though, eh? Never mind, I'm sure we can figure something out.'

The small silence which descended was broken by the arrival of the Tiger.

'Hello, Malik. What, no Khan yet?' He looked at his watch. 'Oh well, another fifteen minutes to go. So, how many scalps for our warrior today, Patel?'

It took Mr Malik only a few minutes to explain to the Tiger the salient points of that day's proceedings, the salientest being that his notebook had been stolen.

'Well, think back. *Aequam memento rebus in arduis servare mentem.* How many do you think you saw?'

'I'm pretty sure I'd counted seventeen new ones. But I can't even remember now if I actually saw that black-fronted bush-shrike. I know I heard it, but . . .'

'Hmm, tricky, very tricky. I'm trying to think what the rules have to say. Do the rules say anything about notebooks, Mr Patel?'

'I don't think so, Tiger. I'll check.'

'And where's Khan? If he doesn't get here soon . . .'

At that moment a screech of brakes from without followed by an excited buzz from within announced Harry's arrival. He entered the bar waving several sheets of Hilton Hotel notepaper, heavily inscribed. Mr Malik's situation was immediately explained, together with the difficulties that the loss of the notebook might entail.

'Difficulties, what difficulties? If Malik says he saw seventeen new species, then that's what he saw. I don't see the problem.'

'But we need the names, you see Khan,' said Mr Patel. 'We need the names to make it official, and so that we'll know that he's really seen them and that they haven't already been seen. I need to record them, to write them down.'

'Oh, I'm sure Malik will remember them eventually. But speaking of writing down names . . .'

Harry Khan thrust the sheets of hotel notepaper into Mr Patel's hands.

'How many, Harry?' came a shout from the bar.

Harry Khan turned to face the room.

'Well, the Committee will have to check it, of course, but I made it . . . now, was it seventy-four or was it seventy-five?'

The lovely island of Lamu had exceeded even George and David's expectations. Only yards from the aircraft steps at the airport on Manda Island they had been dive-bombed by a spur-winged plover. Pearl-breasted swallows swooped low over the grass beside the runway, and as they made their way across the tarmac towards the airport building they almost tripped over a small flock of violet-backed starlings. Outside the building a colony of yellow-backed weavers were chirping and squabbling on a large weeping bougainvillea while two pairs of dusky turtle doves cooed their sad four-note disapproval from a nearby telephone wire. From the boat on the way over to Lamu Island they identified six species of gulls and terns, and watched an osprey speed low over the water, reach down with its talons and pluck a silver fish from just below the surface. A brown and white fish eagle flew slow circles overhead.

It had been no trouble at all to find and hire a small motor-ized fishing boat for the morning. From beneath its canvas awning the three birdwatchers watched egrets wading and cormorants and darters perched on branches over the water drying their wings. They were lucky with the tide. It was going out, so they asked the friendly boatman to take them over to the south end of the island where more waders were feeding on the mud-banks – redshanks, greenshanks, whimbrels, turnstones, sandpipers, golden and Kentish plovers. In the first three hours they recorded fifty-seven species.

'I think we've struck gold, Harry,' said David.

'I think I'm hungry,' said George.

'Lunch,' said Harry, 'is on me.'

The afternoon, though less active, had been almost as productive. After a long lunch at Petley's they stretched out on the grass by the old town wall. Swifts scythed the blue air above them with scimitar wings.

'Eurasian swifts, the big ones,' said George, shading his eyes with one hand and pointing skywards with the other, 'and the smaller ones are little swifts – right, Davo?'

'Yeah. And those two, a bit lower down, with much narrower wings, they must be palm swifts. And hallo. Look at that one, George.'

Binoculars were trained on a bird that looked at first sight like one of the larger Eurasian swifts.

'What do you reckon?'

'I think you could be right, Davo. Yes, I saw the throat. Did you see it, Harry?'

'The one with the white bit, you mean? What is it?'

'Horus swift. The book says you don't usually see one of those so far north but there's no mistaking it.'

And what with the Horus swift, and several kinds of swallows and martins, and the small flock of African spoonbills that flew straight overhead in tight V-shaped formation, their banjo-shaped beaks held out straight before them, George and David and Harry thought they might just as well stay lying on the grass for the rest of the afternoon. By the time they had to leave Lamu and catch the ferry back to the airport the day's tally stood at seventy-four.

'Not bad, not bad at all,' said George, after they had checked into the flight and were waiting at the gate to board the plane. 'But do you know what I'd really like to have seen? A carmine bee-eater.'

A flash of red shot from a railing on the control tower, paused in mid-air to snatch some insect in flight, and glided back towards its perch.

White Pelican

23

Is it an endearing quirk among European explorers to imagine that every geographical feature they clap eyes on for the first time is in need of a new name, or is it just a plain silly one? As far as I understand it, humans have been knocking around this part of Africa for – give or take a birthday candle – three million years. The existence of a large wet patch smack in the middle of them had not gone unnoticed. How large? Bigger than Lake Michigan, bigger than Tasmania, bigger than Connecticut, Massachusetts, Vermont and Rhode Island all rolled into one. It is so big that people on one side gave it one name, people on the other side gave it another and people in between gave it several more. But that didn't matter to Dr Livingstone. Along he came and he didn't ask the locals what they called this large lake at the top end of the Nile. He gave it yet another name, in honour of the elder of a tribe of white people on a small island five thousand miles away. Endearing, or silly? I really can't decide.

Later that night back at the Hilton, Harry – with seventy-five

Lamu notches on his belt – sat down with George and David to plan their next trip.

'I'm thinking west,' said George, taking a meditative sip of Johnnie Walker while looking at the map already spread out on the table.

'West, eh?' said Harry. 'How far west?'

'As far as you can go. Lake Victoria. There should be a few birds round there.'

'Flamingoes,' said David, scanning through his guidebook. 'Greater and lesser.'

'Pelicans, perhaps?'

'White definitely, pink-backed probably.'

'And . . . ?'

'And storks and herons and cranes and rails and ducks and geese and swamp hens and . . .'

'Victoria,' said Harry, 'I think you could be our girl.'

It came to pass that on the third evening Harry Khan returned from the great lake in the middle of Africa, the source of the Nile and a wonder to all men, with a list of birds that included (according to Mr Patel's careful reckoning) no fewer than thirty new species. And there was great rejoicing in the bar, but some consternation. For it was now forty-five minutes past seven and there was still no sign of Mr Malik. Even though he had lost his car the previous day it was unlike him to be late. Where was he?

Mr Malik had not got up at six o'clock that morning to catch the early plane to the town of Kisumu beside Lake Victoria. He had not engaged a driver and car to take him to where the Nzioa River disgorged its water into the lake, and there seen flamingoes (greater and lesser), pelicans (white and spotted) and storks (black, white, woolly-necked, saddle-billed, boat-billed, open-billed and yellow-billed). Neither had he seen a yellow-billed duck, a black duck, a ferruginous duck, a tufted duck, a white-backed duck nor tree ducks – fulvous or white-faced – nor a dozen other species of birds not yet on his list. Indeed, as far as ticking off species on the official checklist of the birds of Kenya goes, Mr Malik's day had been a dud.

I don't know what you would have done if you'd had your car stolen in these circumstances, but with the possibility of holding in my arms the woman of my dreams I would have gone out and hired another. Car hire is expensive in Nairobi but it can be done – Harry Khan is driving round in a hired red Mercedes convertible, is he not? But Mr Malik had lost not only his car and notebook but his wallet, and in his wallet was his driving licence.

I have already alluded to the time it takes to report a crime in Nairobi. This is as the blink of an eye compared to the time it takes to obtain a replacement driving licence. Without a licence Mr Malik could not hire a car. Of course, he could always have called upon the assistance of God.

I was brought up in the Church of England, but it wasn't until I went to Kenya that I first met God. It was my friend Kennedy who introduced us. Needing a telephone line connected to my house in Nairobi I was dismayed to find that some friends who were also recent arrivals had been waiting ten months for such a service and still no telephone.

'Why don't you have a word with God?' said Kennedy. 'I'll give you his number.'

I dialled the number from his house and on the seventh attempt connected (I remember thinking at the time that the seven must have some divine connotation, only to discover later that this is the average number of times one has to dial to be connected in Nairobi).

'Hello,' said God, and it was a revelation. Because God sounded exactly like God should sound. I'd never thought about it before. Growing up with the European imagery of God I'd been happy thinking of him as white, male, venerable and bearded, but I'd never thought about how he might sound if I spoke to him. Like a rabbi, like the Pope, like Orson Welles? I was delighted to find that he in fact sounded like a deep-voiced, Oxbridge-educated

Englishman. He sounded just like the God of the Church of England should sound, and I must say I found this very reassuring. When I later met God at his spacious flat just off South Parade (lovely furniture, and he had a much bigger place in the country, he assured me) I discovered that God is in fact in his thirties, charming, black and gay. And for a fee (donation? offering?) he was able to get my phone connected within a week.

'Ah yes,' nodded Kennedy on hearing the news. 'God works in mysterious ways, his wonders to perform.'

This little detour into telephones and personal revelation is all by way of illustrating that in Kenya there are always alternative ways of doing things. Mr Malik could, if he so chose, have called upon the assistance of my God or any one of a number of other gods to speed his driving licence replacement along. He could, if he so chose, have gone to a hire car company, explained his predicament and discovered that for a small extra fee the legal requirement for producing a driving licence could be waived. But Mr Malik would not do this, because – as we have discovered – Mr Malik is an honest man.

Lying can get you in an awful mess but it isn't easy being honest. Someone shows you a photograph of their new grandchild and says, 'Isn't he just adorable?' Your frank opinion is that if a freshly skinned monkey is adorable then so is this child – but do you say so? If someone near and dear to me were to parade before me in a new dress and ask, 'Does this make my bottom look big?' would I say, 'Yes!'? No. Though Mr Malik had never been put in the latter quandary (the late Mrs Malik, like many women in Africa, did not have so strange and modern an attitude to female proportions), he had been shown more than a few baby photographs in his time to which even he accepted that an honest response would be ill-judged. But despite such occasional lapses Mr Malik's general policy was honesty in all things. In business his word was his bond. If he said he was going to buy at a price, he bought at that price. If he said he was going to sell at a price, he sold at that price. If he said he was going to supply at a certain specification, that specification would be met or exceeded, and if he said he was going to deliver, he delivered.

Mr Malik was well aware of the way the world worked. Every year the Jolly Man Manufacturing Company needed, like all companies, to be registered and licensed. He was legally required to obtain export permits from the Ministry of Trade and bond clearances from the Ministry of Finance. Every employer in Kenya knows that the Immigration Department has the power to close down a business while it makes spot checks for illegal workers, and the Home Security Department now has similar powers. The Ministry of Health could have shut down his factory if there was a suspicion of any of a number of gazetted communicable diseases among his staff. His factory could by law only operate with an annual safety inspection from the Health and Safety department of Nairobi City Council. The Pest Control Department had similar powers, while the Police Department had a hundred ways of making life difficult if they so chose. Mr Malik was diligent in abiding by all the rules, but knew that rules were so often a matter of interpretation. Though he might fill in all the forms, forms can get lost. Just like the telephone company, any regulatory body with any power in Kenya runs two services – a formal one to process the paperwork, and an informal one to ensure the paperwork is processed. If you expect your forms not to get lost and rules to be correctly interpreted, you are expected to pay for both. Mr Malik did not like doing it – was not part of the reason he wrote his 'Birds of a Feather' column to break the cycle of endemic corruption that still stifled freedom and justice in so many aspects of life in Kenya? But at the moment that was the way things worked. That was business. Daily life was another thing. Mr Malik refused to pay a bribe to replace a driving licence, or pay extra to hire a car illegally without one. Highly principled? Unrealistically virtuous? Incorrigibly stubborn? Take your pick.

But it still left him on Monday morning with no car.

Hoopoe

24

On learning of the car theft Mr Malik's daughter Petula had shown more anger than sympathy.

'What were you thinking of, Daddy, walking around in that place? Alone, and with binoculars round your neck for goodness' sake? Why not just have a big sign – Rob Me? Oh, Daddy, Daddy, Daddy.'

She shook her head as her mother used to shake her head at the children when they had done something silly and Mr Malik thought, 'So, it has come to this. Now I am the child and she is the mother. It is strange how things work out.' He asked her to take him to town to buy a new pair of binoculars.

'Look, I'll drop you on my way to work. But please, please promise me you'll take a taxi home.'

Mr Malik agreed and she dropped him in Freedom Street. In the window of Amin and Sons General Emporium he saw a pair of Bausch & Lomb 7 x 50s, and as Godfrey Amin himself was in the shop at the time, as well as getting a good price on the binoculars he stayed for a cup of tea and a chat.

Mr Malik recounted the story of how his car was stolen.

'Oh, and by the way, Godfrey, do you have any notebooks?'

There is very little that you cannot find at Amin and Sons. Mr Malik was shown a number of notebooks of various sizes, lined and unlined, cover stiff or cover floppy. He chose one with a blue cover just like the one that had been stolen, and bought it.

'May I ask what it is for?' said his host.

'Oh, just for jotting down things, you know.'

And it wasn't until he said this that the full horror struck him. The notebook.

If you have ever had the sensation of a heavy weight – a large green coconut, say – falling from a considerable height straight into the pit of your stomach you will know how Mr Malik felt at that moment. The notebook. The one that was stolen. It didn't just have his bird lists. It contained the notes of every conversation he had had with Mr Nyambe over the last five months. If that notebook got into the wrong hands . . .

Mr Malik had heard rumours of bodies being buried in concrete on construction sites administered by the Minister of Housing. People passing the Treasury building after dark had reported muffled screams and remained unconvinced that these were cries of joy from members of staff working late to correct accounting errors. It did not pay to get on the wrong side of those in power. Fumbling for his stiff new wallet and thrusting a handful of notes towards a startled Godfrey Amin, Mr Malik grabbed the bag containing new notebook and binoculars and headed for the door. What was he to do? He needed time to think.

A taxi was waiting outside. He wrenched open the door.

'Where to, sir?'

Where to? What to do? So many questions.

'Just drive on,' he said. A quiet place, somewhere where he could think. The cemetery? No, not the cemetery.

'The arboretum,' he said, slamming shut the door. 'Take me to the arboretum.'

The Nairobi Arboretum, on the other side of town from City Park, is indeed a quiet place. Set up in the 1920s by the colonial government to test which foreign trees might acclimatize to the area, it features specimens from all corners of the world. It also features Christians. I don't know why this few acres behind the university attracts Christians but it does and it doesn't have to be a Sunday – any old day will do. The Christians of Nairobi Arboretum don't seem to be gregarious sorts of Christians. Though you may come across a lot of them you come across them singly, and you might find one almost anywhere – be it in the shadow of a Canary Island palm or an English oak or an Australian gum tree. But you most often see one standing alone in plain view in the middle of the lawn. With Bible or prayer book in hand he or she will be keeping up a steady conversation with God, which from the outside always seems to be pretty much one-way but who knows? And they seem to keep the robbers away.

I should qualify that statement. An uncle of mine who lived near Godalming used to work in the City, taking the train up to town each morning and usually completing the *Times* crossword around about Long Ditton (Clapham Junction on a bad day). At one time, he told me, he occasionally shared his first-class compartment with a chap who used to read *The Daily Telegraph* – a much easier crossword, of course, but otherwise fairly unobjectionable. What *was* objectionable, or at the very least disconcerting, was this fellow's habit, every time he had finished reading a page of the newspaper, of tearing off the top corner, rolling it into a little ball, and throwing it out of the window. At last my uncle could stand it no longer.

'Look here, old chap,' said he. 'I hope you don't mind me asking, but why do you do that? Why do you tear off the corner of every page of your *Daily Telegraph*, roll it into a little ball, and throw it out of the window?'

'Oh, didn't you know?' said this chap. 'It keeps the elephants away.'

The reply set my uncle somewhat aback.

'But my dear fellow, there aren't any elephants in Surrey.'

'No,' said the chap, tearing off another corner. 'Effective, isn't it?'

Which is really just by way of saying that the absence of robbers from the arboretum may not be an effect of the presence of the Christians at all. The two conditions may be causally unrelated or indeed the reverse may even be true. But whether Christians deter robbers or the absence of robbers attracts Christians or there is something else entirely that accounts for both conditions, the fact remains that compared with City Park, Nairobi Arboretum is a haven of peace and rectitude.

Mr Malik asked his taxi driver to wait in the car park. He wasn't planning to go far – just find a bench, sit down and think. He pushed open the green gate, turned left at the big sequoia and headed towards a grove of lemon-scented gums. And blow me down if he didn't see, on the path right in front of him, a hoopoe.

Several years ago my sister gave me a very fine present. It is a centre spread taken from the *Boys' Own Magazine* of 1927, on which, arrayed among a fanciful landscape of trees, river, beach and fields, is every bird that can be seen in Britain. The robin, the blackbird, the thrush and the wren are there, as well as less common birds like the water ouzel and Montagu's harrier. Among the nearly three hundred species represented (it is a very crowded picture) are birds that are not resident in Britain but are occasional visitors – a snowy owl from the Russian tundra, a cattle egret from the Camargue. And there on the ground, jostled between a lapwing and what I'm pretty sure is meant to be a fieldfare, is a hoopoe.

I have never seen a hoopoe in Britain – they are what are known to ornithologists as 'infrequent visitors' – but the first time I saw one in Africa I had much the same feeling as Mr Malik was having now. It was one of happy elation. There is something about the shape of the bird, with its long curved beak and clown's crest, and the colour of the bird, with its bright russet plumage speckled with bands of black and white – there is even something about the very name of the bird – that just cheers you up. Forget the bluebird of happiness, give me a hoopoe every time. It didn't seem at all afraid. It cocked its head to one side, looked up at him with bright black eye. Don't worry, the bird seemed to be saying. Your secret is safe. Don't worry. Mr Malik reached into his pocket for a pencil, opened the new notebook to the first page and wrote down 'Hoopoe'.

Monday at the Asadi Club is usually a quiet night. It is the night when the click of billiard balls is at its most sporadic, when the bar staff have time to polish glasses and catch up on the weekend gossip, when you can drive into a parking space right next to the door. Not so this Monday. It was as well Mr Malik arrived by taxi – had he been driving his own car he would have had to park on the street. The car park was full and the joint was jumping. He paid the taxi driver and made his way to the barroom where he found Mr Patel and Mr Gopez surrounded by an excited crowd of members. Mr Patel was hunched over his lists and standing smiling beside him was Harry Khan.

'Hey, Jack,' he called out. 'How did your day go?'

Mr Malik took the notebook from his pocket and held it up.

Mr Patel, looking up from his table and waving a greeting to his friend, said, 'Khan, thirty.' He stood, and in a louder voice announced, 'Khan, thirty. In total, one hundred and eight.'

Mr Malik pushed his way through the roaring crowd. Without a word he handed Mr Patel his new notebook.

Mr Patel sat down and opened it. He looked silently up at Mr Malik. The crowd became silent. He again got to his feet.

'Malik,' he said in a soft voice, 'one.'

He coughed to clear his throat.

'Malik, one,' he announced. 'In total, forty-nine.'

It was true. The only new bird Mr Malik had seen at the arboretum that day had been that solitary hoopoe.

He had, though, seen quite a lot besides.

25

Khan, one hundred and eight; Malik, forty-nine.

Now, something may have been niggling one or two of you. I don't mean the problem with the stolen notebook – I'm sure you spotted long before Mr Malik that if that notebook got into the wrong hands it could mean trouble. I mean that according to the rules of the competition, as drawn up by Tiger Singh and agreed to by all parties, it is behoven to each protagonist not to mention anything of the reasons behind the competition to anyone outside the Asadi Club. What then are we to make of the fact that Harry Khan seems to be doing all his birdspotting with the help of two people who are not members? Has he told them about the competition? If he has, has he broken the rules?

And what about the fact that while Mr Malik is operating alone and unaided, Harry has had the assistance of a couple of increasingly enthusiastic twitchers? Is this kosher, I hear you ask. Is this halal? Can this really be viewed as strict adherence to the letter and spirit of the competition? To find the answer to these questions (and others) we will return to the club.

If someone had cut a banana in half (just an ordinary banana, not a big cooking plantain) and held it up in front of Harry Khan's face, it would only just have covered the grin that now stretched across it. Malik, one? It was high fives and, 'Drinks on me, boys.' As the crowd moved towards the bar with Harry Khan in its midst, Mr Malik sat down beside his friends.

'What happened?' said Patel.

'My very question,' said Mr Gopez.

'Oh, nothing,' said Mr Malik. 'Well, it's a long story.'

'What time does the club close today, A.B.?'

'Monday? Midnight – as usual.'

Mr Patel looked at his watch, then back to Mr Malik.

'Four hours then – long enough?'

Mr Malik smiled. The two half-empty glasses of beer in front of his friends made him realize he was thirsty. He was about to signal for a waiter when Harry Khan burst out of the crowd around the bar carrying a laden tray.

'Here you go guys, something to keep your strength up.'

Five glasses of Tusker were lifted from tray to table. It was unclear who the fifth glass was for until the familiar form of Tiger Singh also appeared from the crowd.

'A most satisfactory evening, gentlemen,' he said. He glanced at Mr Malik and reached for a beer. 'I mean for the club. We don't usually get this kind of a crowd on a Monday. But before we do anything else, Khan here tells me he has a point he wants a ruling on.'

The two of them sat down at the table.

'Gentlemen, your health,' said Harry Khan, raising his glass. 'Yes, what I want to know about is tomorrow. It's Tuesday. The bird walk. Is it on or is it off? Can we go or can't we?'

'I don't see why not,' said Patel.

'I do,' said Mr Gopez.

'Hmmm,' said the Tiger. 'This could, I fear, be a case of *adhuc sub judice lis est*. I think that the Committee needs to discuss it. Mr Patel, you have a copy of the rules? Come, gentlemen.'

The three members of the Special Committee left our two protagonists sitting alone while they retired to a separate table. Mr Gopez put forward the problem as he saw it.

'The first problem is the lady. The agreement clearly states that neither party is to contact the lady at the heart of the matter until that matter has been resolved. If going on a bird walk on which said lady is present is not contact I don't know what is.'

'I see your point, of course, A.B.,' said the Tiger, 'but you will in fact find that the term "contact" is closely defined.' He turned to the second page of the agreement. '"Both parties also agree that between now and the moment when the Wager is settled, neither will initiate contact – personal, telephonic or epistolary, nor through any third person nor by any other means – with the aforementioned lady." It seems to me that as long as they don't actually talk to her or slip her a billet-doux there's no reason at all why they shouldn't go on the beastly bird walk. What do you think, Patel?'

Patel sat back in his chair.

'Tricky. When is contact contact? A dilemma worthy of a US president, wouldn't you say?'

'Come on, Patel,' said Mr Gopez. 'We're the bloody Committee. We'll just say no and that's that.'

'We are indeed the Committee, A.B., as I'm sure Tiger would agree. And that as the Committee our job is to discuss points as they arise.'

'But never mind if they do promise not to contact her, what would be the point of them going? If they both go, they'll both see the same jolly birds and neither of them will be any better off anyway.'

'I think you're missing something here, A.B. The point at issue – correct me if I'm wrong here, Tiger – is not whether they should go, but whether the rules say they can go.'

'Can go, should go – don't be so namby-pamby. Just tell them they can't go.'

The Tiger thought it time to interject.

'My suggestion, gentlemen, is this. In such a case, I can see no reason why we shouldn't consult with the parties. If both agree, fine. If one disagrees, then it's off. What do you say?'

'Sounds good to me,' said Patel.

'Oh, all right,' said Mr Gopez.

'We should do it separately, though,' said Patel. 'It's important that neither should feel pressured.'

'Absolutely,' said the Tiger. 'We'll hear their views, then give our decision. Now, who shall we have over first?'

There are no prizes for guessing Mr Malik's view on the matter. Just because he had embarked on this bizarre competition and just because he had lost his notebook, did not mean he could forget about his 'Birds of a Feather' column, for which his regular briefing from Thomas Nyambe was, as the Tiger might have said, a *sine qua non*. He was also able to assure the Committee that there was little chance of Rose Mbikwa being there. He remembered that she had said she would be away that week and it was unlikely that she would have changed her mind. He gave the Committee his opinion that either or both parties should be able to go on the bird walk. It was now up to Harry Khan to make his decision.

Harry had to do some fast figuring, and the way he figured was this. Whether Rose was there or not was immaterial. He was well ahead and had been getting further ahead for each of the last two days. Now, if both he and Malik went on the bird walk tomorrow, then presumably they would both see the same birds and at the end of the day he would still be ahead by the same margin. So at the very least it was a safe option. But if neither of them went on the bird walk and he went somewhere new again with David and George (they had already talked about Lake Magadi as a possibility) he had a good chance of getting even further ahead. On the other hand he had to admit he had been getting a little bit worried about the George and David thing. The rules didn't say you couldn't get help to find birds, but they didn't specifically say it was OK. There was just a possibility that he might be caught out here. But if he and Malik went on the bird walk tomorrow, where everyone was helping everyone else, the problem would be solved. They would both have openly benefited from the help of other people in finding birds and there could be no future objection to any help he might get or had been getting from anyone else. That made a lot of sense – yeah, a lot of sense.

'Yeah,' said Harry. 'If it's OK with Jack it's OK with me – hey, I remembered the name.'

The Committee announced its decision, the Tiger went back to the billiard table and Mr Malik sat down with Mr Gopez and Mr Patel in their usual seats.

'By the way, Malik, A.B. and I were wondering,' said Mr Patel, reaching for his glass. 'What's all this "Jack" business?'

'My goodness,' said Mr Malik, standing up again, 'is that the time?'

Starling

26

Though the hoopoe was the only bird that Mr Malik had recorded from his visit to the arboretum, it had not been the only one he had seen. Sparrows fossicked and fought around the rubbish bins. A gang of glossy starlings swaggered across the lawn, on the lookout for worms or other unlucky invertebrates. Red-eyed doves fluttered among the bamboo groves cooing their simple though tedious message, 'I am – a red-eyed dove. I am – a red-eyed dove.' But these were just the usual common or garden birds – none that Mr Malik did not already have on his list.

Was that a regal sunbird flitting among the lemon-scented gum leaves? Mr Malik raised the new binoculars to his eyes. No, not enough red on the chest. It must be a male shining sunbird – he'd seen plenty of those before. But no matter that it wasn't a new species for his list, it was still a pretty little thing. The tiny bird flew over to a flame tree and, ignoring the young man who was rocking back and forth beneath murmuring prayers to the lower branches, began sipping nectar from one of the bright red flowers with its long beak. Off the path to the left, a young woman was conversing with a jacaranda (the Christians of the arboretum, he had already noticed, were as usual out in force). The path to the right led down to the river. Between them, a third path led to the araucaria grove. There was another seat there, a quieter place where he would be able to sit and think more clearly about the stolen notebook. He took the middle way.

Many of you will be familiar with the family Araucariaceae, the group of southern hemisphere trees whose members include the monkey puzzle tree of South America *Araucaria araucana*. The family also boasts several Australian species, and it was towards one of these – *Araucaria bidwillii*, the bunya bunya of southern Queensland – that Mr Malik now bent his steps.

What, he mused as he meandered, should he do? He brushed away some spiky leaves from the empty bench beneath the tree. What *could* he do? The answer seemed clear. Absolutely nothing. And perhaps the hoopoe had been right. Even suppose one of the thieves had read the purloined notebook – and that would have to suppose that any of them could read at all – they would make nothing of its contents. It did not contain his name, nor that of his friend Mr Nyambe. How could they know that the marabou so often referred to was the Minister for Defence? That the vulture was the Minister for Security? And even if, by some remote possibility, they put two and two together, why should they do anything about it? But on the other hand, perhaps the hoopoe had been wrong . . . It was just as he was about to sit down and try once more to reassure himself that the tree spoke.

'Hi,' said the bunya bunya. There was no trace of an Australian accent.

Mr Malik's first reaction was naturally to ignore it.

'Hi,' said the tree again. 'Mr Malik, is that you?'

It is disconcerting to be spoken to by a tree. It is doubly so when that tree clearly recognizes you but you have absolutely no recollection of ever being introduced to the tree. Mr Malik was beginning to feel on shaky ground here. He rose to his feet and began to walk away.

'Mr Malik, please, I need some help.'

Now that he was a little distance away the voice seemed to be coming from about halfway up the tree. When he looked up he saw a black face looking down from the high branches, a face that was clearly human, a face that he recognized. He could see only the face, the body being obscured by foliage.

'Benjamin,' he said with some relief. 'What on earth are you doing up there?'

He had often wondered where the boy went on his regular Monday morning off.

'I climbed up here.'

'Are you stuck?'

'Not stuck, Mr Malik, but I need some help. I can't get down.'

This didn't seem to make any sense.

'Why can't you get down?'

'Because I don't have any clothes on.'

Mr Malik was not sure that this made any more sense.

'Why?' he said.

'I took them off.'

'You took off your clothes, and climbed the tree?'

'No, no, Mr Malik, it was not like that at all,' said Benjamin. 'I climbed the tree first, then I took my clothes off.'

'Why?' he said again.

'He said that I should, the young Christian man. He said that when he wanted to get closer to God he climbed a tall tree.'

'Without any clothes on?'

'He said that if I wanted to get truly close to God I must take off all my clothes, like Adam in the Garden of Eden.'

'Well, put your clothes back on again and come down.'

'I can't. He said I should cast them away.'

'Well, where are they?'

'He said that he would look after them for me.'

'Well, where is he, this Christian man?'

'I don't know. He went away, many hours ago. He took my clothes, and my shoes too. He has not come back.'

On the scale of the bizarre and improbable this all seemed to Mr Malik to rank high, though considerably lower than a talking tree.

'Mr Malik, can you help me?'

'Yes, Benjamin,' he said. 'I will help you.'

It took him twenty minutes to go home in the taxi, another twenty to find the spare key to Benjamin's room and gather up some clothes. He couldn't find any shoes so he brought along a pair of his own flip-flops. On arriving back at the tree he found that Benjamin refused to descend to the lower branches.

'Someone might see me, Mr Malik. That is why I have stayed up here.'

Mr Malik supposed that the boy had a point. Fifty yards away the young woman was still talking to the jacaranda and a flock of primary school children had just swooped on to the lawn and were heading towards them.

'I can appreciate your difficulty, Benjamin,' he said, 'but there is no way I can climb this tree and give you your clothes. I'm afraid you will just have to come down.'

'Mr Malik, I was thinking you might have a piece of string.'

'A piece of string?'

'Yes. You could throw it up here, and I could let one end down and you could tie my clothes to it. Then I can get dressed and climb down.'

Some half an hour later Mr Malik returned from Amin and Sons General Emporium ('Don't ask, Godfrey, please don't ask') with a ball of sisal string of the required length. It took him several girl-like attempts at throwing the string up to Benjamin, then the end of the string was let down, the clothes were hauled up, and after a few minutes Benjamin descended.

'Thank you, Mr Malik,' he said.

'Not at all,' said Mr Malik. 'Now let's go home.'

It was these events which he had been going to tell his friends about at the club that night – until Harry Khan had mentioned the hated nickname. As he hurried out of the club he thought that perhaps it was as well he hadn't.

Apart from the bit about seeing a hoopoe, they might never have believed him.

Long crested Eagle

27

Thomas Nyambe was surprised the next morning to see his friend Mr Malik pull up outside the museum in a taxi. But there was no time for explanations. At the very moment that Mr Malik finished paying the driver Jennifer Halutu appeared on the steps.

'Welcome, everyone, to the Tuesday morning bird walk.'

Mr Malik's slight disappointment at hearing these words uttered by a voice other than that of Rose was tinged with relief. Her temporary absence certainly made things a lot simpler.

'As many of you will remember, while Rose Mbikwa is away she has kindly asked me to lead the bird walk – if that is all right with everybody.'

There were murmurs of approval. Jennifer might not have Rose's voice projection but she knew a lot about birds and was widely liked.

'I know it's past nine but we will wait a few minutes longer – I see quite a few regulars aren't here yet but with all that rain last night I know the traffic is bad this morning. Then I was hoping we might try the ag station.'

When there was enough transport, the State Agricultural Research Station out at Kichaki was another regular venue for the Tuesday bird walk. The small groups relaxed back into their various conversations. Mr Malik moved to the back of the crowd. He was listening to Patsy King tell Jonathan Evans that the unseasonable precipitation of the previous night was probably due to the same low pressure system that had been causing such mayhem on the coast, when Thomas Nyambe walked over to greet him. They exchanged good mornings.

'Your car is at the garage?' said Thomas Nyambe.

Mr Malik's first impulse was to describe the painful events of Sunday to his friend, but he had second thoughts. There was no need to burden Mr Nyambe with his troubles. Then he had third thoughts.

'Stolen, alas.'

And he explained to his friend what had happened, though not about the notebook. There seemed little point in worrying his friend when nothing could be done about it.

'But as my daughter Petula said, it was my own fault. I should never have been in City Park alone. I got what was coming to me, and I am thankful that it was not something worse.'

'Perhaps it is not up to any of us to judge what should be coming to us, my friend – although I hope I know what is coming to the bad people who stole your car. What were you doing at the park?'

'Well . . .' Mr Malik needed to be careful not to say too much. 'Well, there's a sort of competition at my club – who can see the most kinds of birds in a week.'

There, that didn't give too much away.

'What a splendid idea.'

'Oh, do you think so?'

Thomas Nyambe's grin widened.

'Yes, a lovely idea. It will help people see the beauty around them. So many people don't, you know. How many have you seen?'

'Forty-nine.'

'Forty-nine, that sounds good. Congratulations.'

Their conversation was interrupted by the arrival of Tom Turnbull, whose Morris Minor seemed to have acquired yet another ailment since the previous week and was popping away like a two-stroke lawnmower. Just as he was pulling up beside Patsy King's Land Rover a flash of red and a squeal of brakes announced the arrival of Harry Khan, and the crowd were able to compare for themselves the click-curse-click-curse of Tom Turnbull trying to close the door of the ancient Briton and the solid clunk of a modern German car door. As Harry Khan waved to Mr Malik with a broad smile, Thomas Nyambe turned from the spectacle back to his friend and seemed to read something in his face.

'That man – is he in your club? Is he in the competition too?'

Mr Malik nodded.

'And how is he getting on?'

Mr Malik looked towards the ground.

'One hundred and eight,' he said.

Thomas Nyambe, as usual, just smiled.

'Hey, Malik. Still no car, eh – need a lift?'

He saw that the Australian tourists had come along again.

'Is there room for . . . ?'

'Yeah, room for one more in the back. Jump in, Jack.'

What Mr Malik had been about to ask was whether there might be room for two. He wasn't at all sure he felt like jumping anywhere with Harry Khan.

'Why don't *you* go with him,' he said, ushering his friend towards the red Mercedes. 'I'll find a space somewhere else.'

With the help of Thomas Nyambe's expert directions Harry Khan and his party arrived at the ag station ahead of the others, though they didn't have long to wait. Thomas Nyambe was relieved to see that Mr Malik had indeed found a lift in the front seat of Tom Turnbull's Morris with four YOs squeezed in the back. After the group had assembled just inside the gate they wandered up past the pond towards the coffee fields, spotting early along the way a large purple gallinule making a determined but unsuccessful attempt not to be noticed among the reeds, and a bullfinch weaver who didn't seem to mind who saw it pulling strands from a dead rush to make its nest. Mr Malik asked his friend how his own week had been going. And after news had been exchanged of parents and children and grandchildren, he turned to the second page of his new notebook (already adorned with the now customary rough biro sketch of a black eagle on the cover) and began to record the rumours, stories and scandals for what would become the next 'Birds of a Feather' column.

What with the mud created by last night's rain the going was a little slow – it was surprising how often Patsy King had to hold on to Jonathan Evans' shoulder to avoid slipping. The high point of the walk was the sighting of a long-crested eagle sitting on a tree branch with what appeared to be the tail of a rat dangling from the corner of its beak. Judging by the bird's somnolent condition, the rest of the rat was being digested within.

'But for this competition of yours,' said Thomas Nyambe. 'Will you be going somewhere special this afternoon?'

'Oh no, not this afternoon.' Mr Malik tapped the notebook. 'I have some writing to do.'

'Of course – how silly of me. But tomorrow?'

Yes, where would he go tomorrow? Mr Malik really hadn't thought about it.

'I don't know,' he said. 'It's a bit difficult without a car.'

'I wondered, have you thought about the sewage works?'

'No, why?'

'Oh, you never know what you'll see at the sewage works. We used to go there a lot a few years ago, but people didn't like the smell. What with the weather and all it might be worth trying, especially at this time of year.'

Though Mr Malik couldn't see what the recent rain had to do with the abundance of avifauna at the Nairobi sewage works, he said nothing.

'I suppose you'd have to take a taxi,' said Mr Nyambe, and smiled a big smile, 'but I think you'll find the cost might be worth it. And give me the registration number of your car. I'll ask the other drivers to keep a lookout. You never know.'

While Mr Nyambe continued to fill Mr Malik in on the latest government gossip the two friends drifted slightly away from the main group. Their conversation was interrupted by a small sound.

'I say,' said Mr Malik, on hearing the short, high 'peep'. 'That sounds like – yes, it is. Look, a malachite kingfisher.' A flash of blue arrowed towards the pond. The kingfisher perched on a low branch above the water, raised and then lowered a pale blue crest and sat as still as a cat, staring down into the water. With its red bill and the bright orange of its breast it looked like something from a jeweller's window.

'That is indeed a fine bird,' said Mr Nyambe. 'All birds are fine, but that is one of the finest.'

'Yes, I'll call the others over.'

'But what about . . . ?'

Mr Nyambe did not finish his question. Of course, the others must be called. Including Harry Khan.

Mr Patel determined that the bird walk that morning had in fact added two new species to Harry Khan's list – while purple gallinule and long-crested eagle were already on it, so far he hadn't seen a bullfinch weaver or a malachite kingfisher (it was good, thought Harry, that all those other people had been there to point the birds out to him – to them both). He accepted the additions to his master list with a grin, waved to the crowd and headed for the door.

'Wait wait wait,' said Mr Gopez. 'You can't leave yet; Malik hasn't arrived. He hasn't had his list checked.'

'Sorry guys, got to go. I'm sure you can deal with Malik, no problem.'

'Wait wait wait *wait*,' said Mr Patel. 'What we mean is, you *have* to stay. It's the rules.'

'I don't think so, boys. I got a hot date, I got to make tracks.'

'Tiger, tell him – it's in the rules, isn't it?' said Mr Gopez. 'Tell Khan here he's got to wait for Malik.'

The Tiger looked up from the billiard table where he was lined up for a tricky cannon off two cushions.

'No, I don't think he does. I don't think the rules say he has to stay. He can go if he wants to.'

'Great. See you tomorrow then, guys.'

As Harry Khan pulled out of the club car park he saw a taxi coming in. So, Jack hadn't got his car back yet.

'Wasn't that Khan just leaving?'

Mr Malik dropped his notebook on to the table by the bar and flopped down into a chair beside it.

'Yes, he said he couldn't wait. Hope that's all right with you.'

'Perfectly,' said Mr Malik.

'Saw a few new ones on the bird walk today then, did you?' said A.B. 'Khan told us you'd both been, but he only got two. How many did you see?'

'Just one, I think.'

Which was quite true. With the exception of the malachite kingfisher all that day's birds were already on Mr Malik's list.

'You're really going to have to do better than that, old chap. If you asked me I'd say it was time to pull the old finger out.'

'Yes, I'm sure you're . . .'

'Only three days to go. That makes Khan one hundred and ten and you on fifty.'

'Yes,' said Mr Malik. 'I know.'

African
Emerald
Cuckoo

28

'Still no car, I see,' said Mr Patel.

It was Wednesday evening, and Mr Malik had once more been forced to take a taxi to the club.

'No. Has Harry Khan been in?'

'Yes,' said Mr Gopez. 'He said he couldn't wait again. Hope that's all right with you.'

'Of course,' said Mr Malik, taking his new notebook from the pocket of his jacket and putting it on the table. 'How did he get on?'

'How many was it, Patel? Ten new ones?'

'Twelve, A.B. – a hundred and twenty-two in total. I told you that you needed to pull the old finger out, Malik. I'm afraid he's rather pulling away.'

'Twelve, eh. Where did he go?'

'Lake Naivasha, apparently,' said Mr Gopez.

'Lake Naivasha *and* Hell's Gate,' said Mr Patel. 'What about you?'

'Oh, just the sewage works.'

'The sewage works?' said Mr Patel.

'The sewage works?' said Mr Gopez.

'The sewage works, old man?' said Tiger Singh, loudly, from the bar.

'It's all down there,' said Mr Malik gesturing to his notebook still on the table. 'And while you gentlemen add up how many new species I saw – at the sewage works – I think I will order myself a beer.'

'Need to get the taste out of your mouth, eh Malik?' said Mr Patel. 'All right, let's see how you did today.'

He reached for Mr Malik's notebook, opened it and began counting.

I suppose there must be some disadvantages to being a bird. Having no lips or teeth, for instance, presents severe limitations to facial expression – and no doubt to the clear enunciation of some of the fricative consonants. With no thumb or fingers to speak of a bird might find it somewhat tricky to bowl a good leg spin. And while feathers are all very well for forming aerodynamic surfaces and are wonderful insulation, they probably tend to get a bit stuffy on a warm day. But the really good thing about being a bird (with no disrespect to any ostriches, emus or penguins who may be reading this) is that you can fly.

Suppose you were a crab, say, down at the coast. A big storm comes up, what do you do? Dig a deep hole and hope for the best, I suppose. But if you're a bird, you just look at those big black clouds coming towards you, spread your wings and scoot off in the other direction. If you happened to be on the coast of Kenya when a big storm came in from the east you'd naturally head west. After a couple of hours flying you might be looking for somewhere to rest. Oh, what's that down there? Is that a series of large ponds I see – some full of water, some full of nice wet mud? Why, that looks like just the place to take a break and maybe find a worm or two. And down you glide. Which is why when a big storm breaks on the Kenya coast one of the

137

very best places to see birds is the Nairobi municipal sewage works.

Mr Malik had taken Mr Nyambe at his word and ordered an early taxi. When he got to the sewage works it seemed that every bird from the entire coast of East Africa had already arrived. Waders were there in thousands – blacksmith plovers standing statuesque beside the ponds, whimbrels and godwits probing the mud with scimitar beaks, sandpipers bobbing through the shallows flashing little white bottoms by the score. Dozens of herons and egrets were stabbing the water for fish or insects. Huge flocks of cormorants were packed together, large and small, swimming and diving. Gulls and terns were swooping and squabbling, ducks were dabbling and geese paddling. There were even – and Mr Malik had to take the binoculars from his eyes and rub them twice before checking again – three large pink flamingoes.

Mr Malik remembered the first time he had seen a flamingo. It had been in 1955, just before he started at Eastlands High. His parents had taken the family for a weekend club outing to Lake Borgoria. As their car topped the low hills and he had his first glimpse of the lake stretching before them, he could see that its whole shoreline was edged with pink. At a single glance he could see not three, not three hundred, not three thousand but a million flamingoes. There was not room in his eleven-year-old imagination for so many birds. But he had never seen a flamingo in Nairobi. As he looked and scribbled and looked and scribbled, he wished his friend Mr Nyambe was with him. Mr Malik would have liked to thank Mr Nyambe for telling him about this place, and he was sure Mr Nyambe would have had almost as much pleasure from seeing all these birds as he was having.

'Haven't you finished counting yet, Patel?'

'Yes, A.B. – and never mind the stench of sewage. Malik old chap, I take it all back. I think we may be smelling the sweet scent of victory here, gentlemen. I make it . . . seventy-four.'

'Don't be ridiculous, Patel. Impossible. I don't believe it.'

'Look for yourself, A.B.'

'You must be getting mixed up, confused. I don't want the total, I want to know how many new ones he's seen today.'

'That's what I'm telling you, seventy-four.'

He went over to the noticeboard, crossed off the previous total and wrote up the new one.

'Khan one hundred and twenty-two, Malik one hundred and twenty-four. Malik takes the lead.'

What had been looking like a one-horse race was now neck and neck.

'Splendid work, Malik,' said Mr Gopez. 'Glad to see you took my advice.'

'Sewage works, though, who'd have thought it?' said Mr Patel, beginning to giggle. 'Must have been stiff with hadadas out there.'

'Never mind that,' called the Tiger. 'It's the numbers that count. Well done, Malik.'

'I suppose someone should tell him,' said Patel.

'I thought we'd just told him,' said Mr Gopez. 'You have been tuning in, Malik? You have been listening to all this, haven't you? You do know you're in the lead?'

'Not him, A.B. – Khan. Someone should tell Khan.'

'Tell him? How can we, he isn't here.'

'I know he's not here. He's gone. So someone should tell him.'

'Tosh. If he must keep going off before Malik arrives, serves him right.'

'I know that, but it's only fair.'

'It doesn't say anything in the rules about telling him.'

'I know it doesn't, but . . . well, what do you think, Tiger?'

'I think A.B.'s quite right,' said the Tiger. '*Ex proprio motu* and all that. There's nothing really in the rules that covers it. Each party agreed to appear here on each evening of the competition – nothing was said about staying.'

'If you will excuse me, gentlemen,' said Mr Malik. 'I just have to make a telephone call.'

The receptionist at the Hilton was told that the caller didn't want to disturb Mr Khan but could he just leave a message. The message was quite short. 'One hundred and twenty-four. Yes, that's all. One hundred and twenty-four.' And Mr Malik had to admit, as he put down the telephone receiver and returned to the bar, that he took some pleasure from that short conversation.

As soon as he received the message Harry Khan knew exactly what those words meant. He called David and George to convene an immediate meeting in the hotel lounge.

'Right,' said David. 'Time to get moving. We've done the coast, we've done the lake, I'm thinking it might be time to head for the hills.'

'I thought we were already in the hills,' said George. 'How high are we here in Nairobi – five thousand feet or something?'

'The mountains, then. Kilimanjaro.'

It was Harry's turn to step in with a little of the geographical knowledge he had picked up from Rose.

'Kilimanjaro, though clearly visible from Nairobi on a good day, is actually in Tanzania. Beyond the bounds, guys. Mount Kenya, though, would that be any good?'

'Perfect,' said David. 'Whole new suite of avifauna, I shouldn't wonder.'

'Montane orioles,' said George, flicking through the bird book. 'White-eyes, Hartlaub's turaco. It says here you've got a fair chance of seeing a lammergeier. Could be a bit tricky doing it all in a day, though. It'll be a fair old drive.'

'Who said anything about driving?' said Harry.

The next morning they were up again at dawn. A small plane was waiting for them at Wilson Aerodrome and by eight thirty they were breakfasting on the veranda of the Mount Kenya Safari Club while the resident wildlife guide went through the day's programme. They might start with a stroll in the club's grounds, then he would take them by Land Rover into the national park. Harry liked the sound of the Land Rover. Even here at the foot of the mountain the air was so thin he had felt distinctly short of breath just climbing the front steps of the club.

With the help of the guide (a guide who had been trained, as you might expect, by Rose Mbikwa) they saw, not a mile from the Safari Club and jousting high above them with a young Verreaux's eagle, a lammergeier. In their first half-hour in the forest a Hartlaub's turaco flew across their path, followed by an African emerald cuckoo, a flock of small brown birds that went by the unlikely name of cinnamon bracken-warblers, as well as mountain warblers, orioles, white-eyes and a host of other altitude-loving species. They even heard, then saw, a nine-banded woodpecker – they counted the bands twice, just to be sure.

Back at the club for a well-earned afternoon tea on the terrace, George pointed out a sunbird with narrow curved bill and two extended tail feathers. It was feeding on a hibiscus by the main steps.

'That's a bronzie, isn't it?' said David.

'Not according to this book.' George held up his bird guide. 'That there little beauty is a Tacazze sunbird. I don't think we've had one of those on the list yet.'

'I'm sure we haven't,' said Harry, writing it down. 'Thank you, George. That makes a nice round . . . fifty. Fifty new species. You know, guys, I think we're in the lead again – well in the lead. Forget the tea, I think something a little more appropriate might be called for. Waiter, a bottle of champagne – Bollinger.'

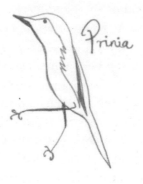

Prinia

29

'Your car, Mr Malik, it's been spotted.'

Mr Malik recognized Mr Nyambe's voice on the telephone. He put down his Nescafé.

'Green Mercedes, licence plate NHI 572? One of our drivers has just radioed in. It's on Valley Road heading for Ngong Road. He'll try and follow it. We'll let you know if it gets parked anywhere. Do you have a spare key?'

Mr Malik confirmed that he had.

'Good. I'll get back to you as soon as I hear anything. Can you stay by the phone?'

Mr Malik had not been planning to stay by the phone. As soon as he finished his morning Nescafé he had intended to visit the hospital. After that he had planned to take a taxi out to the sewage works again – it seemed possible that he had missed the odd species or perhaps some more had turned up. But still, he really did need his car back.

*   *   *

I was never sure whether to believe the stories you used to hear in Nairobi about how the son of a senior high court judge is the man behind most of the car hijackings and car thefts in the city, and how he has close links with certain police officers and at least one member of the government. Nor was Mr Malik, but he half believed it. If by some miracle his car could be found, he would need to be ready. Ready to get to it fast, get into it, and drive away with as little fuss as possible. As for his other plans, well, he would just have to change them. He would wait at home until he got the phone call, get the car, and then go to the hospital. If there was time for birdwatching after that, so much the better. In fact, while he was waiting for the call he may as well look out for birds in the garden.

Mr Malik had settled back into his chair on the veranda with binoculars and notebook ready on the table beside him. A family of mousebirds were playing in the bougainvillea – at least he assumed they were a family and he assumed they were playing. No, he was sure they were a family. He remembered Rose Mbikwa talking about some research that had been done on them, how they stayed in family groups and how last year's young would stay with their parents and help feed and bring up the next brood. As to whether they were really playing, well who could say? But having raised and closely observed two young of his own, Mr Malik had little doubt that the chasing and squabbling of young birds and young humans were just the same. His philosophical musing was interrupted by the sound of sweeping.

'Good morning, Benjamin,' said Mr Malik. He wondered if he should say something about the arboretum.

'Good morning, sir,' said Benjamin.

He too was wondering whether he should mention the arboretum business when his eyes fell on the table. Mr Malik noticed him noticing.

'Ha ha,' he said. He smiled his most beneficent smile. 'Ho ho,' he said. 'No, not hadadas today, Benjamin.' He raised the binoculars. 'Birds in general – all birds.'

It was clear from the look he received that the boy was not completely reassured.

'Look. Over there, see? A sparrow.'

'Ah, yes, sir. *Shomoro*.'

'And there, a mousebird.'

'Ah,' said Benjamin after a small hesitation. 'Yes, sir, *kuzumburu*. *Kuzumburu michirizi*.'

'And another one, over there – see?'

'Ah yes, sir. Different one. *Kuzumburu kisogo-buluu*.'

'Exactly. No, just a minute. What did you say?'

'*Kuzumburu*, sir. That bird. *Kuzumburu kisogo-buluu*.'

'What?'

Benjamin put down his home-built broom.

'That one there, sir,' he said, pointing to the second bird which was now hanging upside-down in a bougainvillea tearing at a purple flower, '*kuzumburu kisogo-buluu*. The other one there, *kuzumburu michirizi*.'

Mr Malik picked up his binoculars. By golly the boy was right. What he'd thought was another speckled mousebird was a blue-naped mousebird. Sharp eyes.

'Thank you, Benjamin. Well spotted.'

'Thank you, sir.'

Benjamin picked up the broom and resumed his sweeping. If the boss really was looking at birds this time he was not making a very good job of it.

'Benjamin.'

Benjamin stopped again. This was going to be where Mr Malik mentioned the arboretum. He looked over to where Mr Malik had now stood up and was holding open a book.

'Come over here for a moment, would you? I'd like to show you something.'

Benjamin leaned his broom against the wall. What would it be – a Bible? No, on every page of the book were pictures of birds, and next to the pictures some writing in English. Mr Malik flicked through the pages and held up one for him to see.

'Do you know these birds?'

Though Benjamin found the pictures a little strange – where was the movement, where were the cheeps and chuckles? – they seemed to be of the three different *kuzumburu* that he had seen around the village when he was growing up.

'Ah yes, sir, *kuzumburu*.' He pointed to each in turn. '*Kuzumburu michirizi*, little bit of white face. *Kuzumburu kisogo-buluu*, little bit of blue here, on the back of the neck. This one here – *kuzumburu kichwa-cheupe* – I have never seen in Nairobi, only sometimes in my village when it has been very dry.'

Mr Malik gave him a long look. He turned to another page. 'And these?'

On the page were pictures of more birds, eaters of meat – not *tai mzoga*, eaters of dead things – but *tai msito* and *kipanga*. He pointed to each and named them.

'What about these?'

Mr Malik turned to a page on which sacred and glossy ibises perched beside an African spoonbill (and as if flapping its brown wings and shouting its three-note call from the top of the page, a hadada). Benjamin duly identified the two *kwarara* with their long curved beaks and the *domomwiko* with its beak like a flattened *borok*.

'Excellent,' said Mr Malik with a broad smile. 'You clearly know your birds, Benjamin.'

'Thank you, sir.'

'I would very much like your help again today, Benjamin. Not with hadadas – we've probably counted enough of those. What I would like you to do is sit with me here on the veranda and show me all the other birds you can see.'

Over the next four hours Mr Malik, who had always thought that only three kinds of sunbirds visited his garden, was surprised to find that with Benjamin's help he could positively identify five. And what he'd thought was a female yellow-whiskered bulbul was really a Fischer's greenbul. The boy had a very good ear for bird calls too. In a small feeding flock that passed through the garden he was able to tell apart by their sounds alone two apalis, a prinia and no fewer than three warblers (with his binoculars Mr Malik was able to positively identify only two of the warblers, but he was sure Benjamin was right). And though Mr Malik was used to hearing owls calling at night he had never realized that a wood owl regularly roosted deep among the foliage of a climbing monstera by his own front gate. If you got in the right position over in the corner of the garden you could just get a glimpse of its distinctive barred breast feathers. But still, no phone call.

It wasn't until five o'clock in the afternoon that the phone finally rang.

'Mr Malik? I'm afraid we lost it. At Dagoretti Corner – at the big roundabout there, you know. We've been looking all round the place but no sign. I'm sorry.'

Chestnut Headed Bee-eater

30

It was Mr Malik who arrived first at the club that Thursday evening.

'Still no car, eh?'

Mr Malik shook a weary head at his friend Patel. No car, and no notebook. The question was repeated by Harry Khan when he arrived at the club a few minutes later, back from his trip to Mount Kenya.

'Sorry to hear that, Jack. And thanks for your message last night. Yeah, thanks.'

Mr Gopez stared at Mr Malik. Mr Patel smiled an inscrutable smile. Tiger Singh spoke.

'I'm glad to see you're both here on time, gentlemen. If you could hand over your notebooks to Mr Patel we'll see what the score is.'

Though confined to his garden all that day while waiting for the phone call, Mr Malik had been surprised to identify – with Benjamin's help – twelve new species. But this was nowhere near Harry's Mount Kenya score. A few minutes later Mr Patel announced the result.

'Malik one hundred and thirty-six. Khan one hundred and seventy-two. Mr Khan is back in the lead. But *dum anima est, spes esse dicitur*, gentlemen. Don't forget, there are still two days left to go.'

In announcing that the wager between Mr Malik and Harry Khan had two more days to run, the Tiger had been uncharacteristically inaccurate. There remained, as both parties were well aware and I'm sure you are too, all of the following day but only half of Saturday. That night at the Hilton, Harry Khan planned his final assault.

'After that trip to Mount Kenya today we're well ahead again, boys, but I want to be further ahead. I want to be so far ahead of Malik that he won't even see me with a spotting scope.'

'We're with you, Harry,' said George, munching on a large olive. 'Right, Davo?'

'Right,' said David. 'I don't know what you two think, but my idea is this. Another one-day safari tomorrow – we've been reading up on this and Kakamega might be a good bet – then up early on Saturday for another try at Nairobi National Park.'

'Yes, Kakamega Forest. Listen to this.' George began reading aloud from his guidebook, ' "Kakamega – remnant of equatorial rainforest which once spanned the continent from west to east – famous for its birds and butterflies – unique combination of lowland and highland species." Now the important part – are you still listening? "Forty-five of the species on the Kenya list are to be found only in the Kakamega."'

'Sounding good, guys.'

'Grey parrot, green-throated sunbird, blue-headed bee-eater, red-chested owlet, grey-chested illadopsis, Ansorge's greenbul, Shelley's greenbul, Chapin's flycatcher, Turner's eremomela . . . the list goes on.'

'Turner's eremomela, eh? Could be our kind of place. How do we get there?'

148

'There's an airstrip a few k's out of town. Charter a plane again, then hire a taxi.'

'OK, guys. Leave it to me.'

'But you know,' said George, sinking back into the soft Hilton sofa, hands behind head. 'Only a day and a half left. It's not long. Shame we can't go birdwatching at night.'

'Why would you want to go birdwatching at night?' said Harry. 'Aren't all good little birds tucked up in their nests or whatever?'

'Not necessarily. You remember, Davo, on that trip to Maasai Mara when we went spotlighting for mammals, just outside the park? We saw a few birds then.'

'Yeah, you're right. We saw those nightjars, the ones with the long tails.'

'Pennant nightjars. And didn't we see an owl?'

'It sounds great, guys,' said Harry, 'but haven't you forgotten? I have to be back in Nairobi by seven.'

'I wasn't thinking of trying it at Kakamega. We still have tomorrow night after you've finished at the club. I'm sure we could find some spotlights before then.'

'And we don't need a national park,' said David. 'What about that place near the MEATI?'

'Good thinking, Davo. We saw a lot of birds there that day. If we got up really early we could start there on Saturday morning before light, then go on to the park as soon as it opens.'

'OK, boys. Sounds good to me,' said Harry. 'We'll give it a go. I'll be seeing Elvira later. I'll tell her to find us a couple of good spotlights tomorrow while we're away.'

If Mr Malik had been disappointed that day at not being reunited with his car, the revelation that evening that Harry Khan had once more pulled ahead in the competition only compounded his despair. And he still couldn't help worrying about that missing notebook. Where was his car, where was his notebook, and where would he find another thirty-seven species of birds before

Saturday noon – another fifty or sixty if his opponent's luck continued the way it seemed to have been going so far? He was also feeling guilty. Thanks to staying at home waiting for that phone call he had missed his visit to the hospital, and for what? For this silly competition. Was it really that important? He had been musing on these questions all night and he was still musing on them the following morning when Benjamin appeared around the corner of the bungalow, freshly made broom in hand.

'Ah, Benjamin,' he said, putting down his cup of Nescafé. 'Thank you again for all your help yesterday.'

It really had been remarkable how many birds those sharp young eyes had spotted.

'More birds today, sir?' said Benjamin.

'Well, I would like to see more birds. But I don't think I'll find many more in this garden, even with your help.'

'No sir, Nairobi is not so good for birds. Even in my village there are more birds.'

'Remind me where your village is, Benjamin.'

'Oh, far away from here, sir. Too far to walk, even in a whole day.'

Mr Malik smiled a small smile and reached for his cup. The telephone rang.

There is something about African time that even the Swiss find a challenge. The Swiss International flight from Zurich had landed at Jomo Kenyatta International Airport the previous evening its usual nine minutes late. Chatting to the taxi driver on the ride from the airport to Serengeti Gardens, Rose Mbikwa discovered that in the nine days she had been away it had rained once, two matatus had collided on the Uhuru Road killing nineteen people, and the Minister for Forests and Fisheries had been forced to resign over the Karura Forest affair. This last item was big news indeed. While scandals and corruption are not uncommon in Kenyan politics (as anyone who reads the 'Birds of a Feather' column in the *Evening News* well knows) Rose could not remember the last time a minister had actually resigned. The taxi driver said it was the story in the paper that started it all. Ah, thought Rose with a sad smile, if only someone had been writing a column like that when Joshua was alive.

The driver turned into Serengeti Gardens and, after successfully negotiating the potholes, unmarked speed bumps and the usual string of cars parked outside the house of her neighbour the high court judge, pulled into her driveway. The eye operation had been successful and she had been well looked after at the clinic but it was good to be back. She went straight upstairs to bed.

Soon after dawn she was awoken by the cry of hadadas and wondered for a moment where she was. Oh yes, Kenya. Home. Slipping on a dressing gown (and not forgetting to put on her eyepatch) she went to the bedroom window and pulled back the curtains. Another bright Nairobi day, though already tinged with the haze of an early bonfire from the street outside. There seemed even more cars out there than ever – perhaps it was time to have a friendly word with her neighbour. How many cars did one judge need? But that would wait. What she really wanted now was a nice long bath. Rose was about to leave the window when something about one of the cars outside on the street caught her eye. Parked between a red four-wheel-drive something or other and a white four-wheel-drive something or other else (apart from Peugeot 504s, Rose was not good on cars) was a vehicle she was sure she recognized.

Still in her dressing gown, she went downstairs and out of the front door.

Flamingo

31

Mr Malik's first reaction on recognizing the voice on the other end of the telephone was total silence.

'Mr Malik? Mr Malik, is that you? This is Rose Mbikwa.'

He took a deep breath.

'Yes, Mrs Mbikwa. I'm so sorry, it is indeed I.'

Why was she telephoning him, and why so early in the morning? She had never phoned him, and didn't she know the rules of the competition for goodness' sake?

'Good. How are you? I must apologize for calling you so early, but I just wondered if you had lost your car.'

Car? How did she know?

'Yes, Mrs Mbikwa. I have indeed lost my car.'

'Well, there's one here outside my house and it looks just like yours. It's a green Mercedes, and it has a sticker on the window – an AIDS Aware one, you know? – and one from the Ornithological Society too. I've got the registration number here – NHI 572.'

'Thank you, Mrs Mbikwa. That is my car. It was stolen last weekend.'

'Yes, I wondered if that might be the case. Such things seem to happen so often in Nairobi these days. What would you like me to do?'

Mr Malik thought fast.

'I think it would be best if I came and got it. I have a spare key. Perhaps if you could tell me where I might find it?'

Rose gave Mr Malik her address and went to run her bath. She had not noticed that AIDS sticker on Mr Malik's car before, though on thinking about it such a thing seemed perfectly in keeping. By the time she had finished her bath and got dressed for the day ahead, the old green Mercedes with the back window stickers was gone. That was strange. She had thought he would have called in.

Back in his chair on the veranda of his house in Garden Lane and over a second cup of Nescafé (an unusual event – he had not drunk more than one cup of Nescafé at breakfast since that dreadful day his wife died), Mr Malik took stock of the situation. He had his car back, though despite searching every crack, corner and crevice he had not found the missing notebook. There was another problem. The rules of the competition were clear; there was to be no contact with Rose Mbikwa – personal, telephonic or epistolary, nor through any third person nor by any other means. He hadn't meant to, but Mr Malik had broken that rule. It had not been him who had called, though, it had been her. He could hardly have slammed down the phone on hearing her voice. Oh well, he'd just have to wait and see what the Committee would say. At least he had been able to retrieve the car without actually seeing her.

But ah, the sound of her voice. The words of an old song came back to him, one he hadn't heard since leaving London in the 1960s – had it been Dusty Springfield? *'I'm in meltdown, I have no choice. Meltdown when I hear your voice.'* That was just how Rose Mbikwa's low contralto on the other end of the line had made him feel. It was how he still felt. Could it be that he might actually win this strange competition? Was it possible that Rose Mbikwa would accept his invitation to the Hunt Club Ball? Was it possible, could it be that he would dance with her, and once more hear her soft voice speak his name?

Birds. He needed more birds. Mr Malik sighed a long sigh, followed by another so loud that Benjamin, who had by this time finished sweeping round the house and driveway and was halfway across the lawn, looked up.

'Ah, Benjamin.'

Was Mr Malik at last going to say something about the arboretum?

'Benjamin, how long have you worked for me now?'

'For five months and a half, sir. Since the end of the little rains.'

'Yes, good. Five months, eh? And on your days off, do you ever go home?'

'No, sir. Not yet, sir. Perhaps soon, when I have saved enough money.'

What with the price of bonbons and Coca-Cola (not to mention having to replace one complete set of clothes – including shoes) Benjamin had been finding it harder than he'd thought to save money in the big city.

'On the bus, how long would it take you?'

'Four hours, sir. That is if there is one puncture. If there are more punctures, perhaps longer.'

'What if there were no punctures?'

'Then not so long, sir.'

What had the boy said about seeing more birds in his village than in Nairobi?

'Benjamin,' said Mr Malik. 'I think it's time you had a holiday.'

Heading out of Nairobi down to the plains and the wide rift valley you can take either the high road or the low road. The high road is newer and better, but being newer and better it takes the most traffic. The low road is narrower and bendier, but you are slightly less likely to encounter an overloaded truck coming at you on the wrong side of the road, or fifty people standing round a bus watching the driver fix that morning's first puncture. Mr Malik chose to take the low road and reached Naivasha just two hours after leaving Number 12 Garden Lane.

It was dry down on the plains, and hot. The long rains had not been good and the short rains were not due for many months. In the fields the maize grew stunted and brown. Nor was there any greenness left in what little coarse grass still stood uneaten by sheep and goats, while the animals themselves stood thin and listless in the sparse shade of the thorn trees. Perhaps it had not been such a good idea to come here. This was no place for birds.

After one more hour of driving north, just after a large sign assuring him that Omo still washes whiter, Mr Malik found himself being directed by an excited Benjamin on to an unmarked dirt road. When they slowed down to allow a scrawny cow and her even scrawnier calf to move aside, the cloud of brown dust that they created behind them caught up with the car. It was some minutes before Mr Malik could see far enough ahead to drive on.

'That is my uncle's cow, sir. When I left here she had no calf. It is good that she has a calf.'

Mr Malik supposed that it was.

'How far now?' he said.

'We are nearly at the school, sir,' said Benjamin. 'After the school, just three miles.'

Eritima Primary School proved to be a one-roomed wooden building just off the road. Behind it was a much smaller building, presumably the schoolmaster's house. To one side was a soccer pitch, only distinguishable from the rest of the bare earth that stretched out all around it by the presence of two crooked wooden goals. Some children seemed to be running a race between them. None of them seemed to be wearing shoes.

'That is my school, sir. That is where I did my learning. It is a very good school. They are practising for sports day.'

'Ah, I see. But why is the school not in the village? Why is it so far away?'

'The electricity, sir. Here there is electricity, but not in the village, not yet.'

Mr Malik could see that the thin power line that they had been following since the turn-off did indeed end at the school-master's house.

They were now heading towards some low hills, bare and brown as the country all around. The road began to climb and got rougher. Mr Malik slowed down, guiding the old Mercedes between boulders and wash-outs.

'There, sir. There is my village.' They had reached the crest of the hill and Benjamin was pointing down into the small valley below. 'That is where I was born. That is where my father and mother live. It is a very good village.'

Mr Malik had been expecting to see a collection of huts surrounded by bare earth and brown dust, like the school back there. But it was not bare and it was not brown. He stopped the car.

Most of the buildings appeared to be along one main street, and behind each was a patch of bright green. More fields of green stretched out down the valley. Some kind of crop must be growing. In countless square miles of arid brown, the little village was a green oasis.

A few minutes later and they were in the village street, surrounded by a crowd of smiles. It seemed to Mr Malik that he was introduced to every man, woman and young child in the village, and that every one of them was Benjamin's father, mother, aunt, uncle, or cousin. He had expected to see a stream or river running through the village – how else to explain the gardens of beans and tomatoes and the crops of maize and sorghum? There was indeed a river, but its course was marked not with rippling water but sand and dry stones.

'The water, Benjamin, where does it come from?'

'From the spring, sir. From the spring beneath the mountain. It is a very good spring. Come, I will show you. That is where we will see the birds.'

Great Blue Turaco

32

The single-engined Cessna 207 Skywagon made a low circle of the small town before touching down at Kakamega airstrip just before nine o'clock. Its appearance over the town had been a signal to the Kakamega's only taxi driver. The plane's three passengers had no more than minutes to wait until a Peugeot 504 – of slightly more recent vintage than Rose Mbikwa's but of similar appearance – arrived to take them to the guesthouse. Built in the 1930s by the local sawmill owner in the shade of one of the few Elgon olive trees he had not yet cut down, cut up and sold, the Kakamega Guesthouse not only does a fine breakfast but is an excellent place to see birds that you will see nowhere else in Kenya – including the strangely named Turner's eremomela.

Ever since 1735 when the Swedish naturalist Carl von Linné published his great *Systema Naturae*, each species of plant and animal has been known to science by a unique binomen, a combination of two words that apply to it and it alone. I, for instance, am a member of the species *Homo sapiens*. You probably are too. The lion is *Panthera leo*, the lamb a junior member of the species *Ovis aries*. Birds are not exempt from Linnaean nomenclature. The black kite, which you may remember meeting at the start of the narrative, is known to ornithology as *Milvus migrans*. The cinnamon-chested bee-eater rejoices in the alter nomen of *Merops oreobates*. Which has all made life a lot easier for ornithologists, who can be absolutely sure that when they are talking to each other about a bird they are talking about the same bird.

Among English-speaking birdwatchers – and a recent UK survey suggests that 87.4% of the birdwatchers worldwide use English as their first language (with a worrying 85.1% using English as their first and only language) – there have been concerted efforts over the years to do the same kind of thing with the *common* names of birds. In the brave new ornithological world thus envisioned, each of the world's 10,000 or so bird species will be given an English common name and only one common name. What might once have been called a merle in Scotland and a blackbird in England will now be officially known as the common blackbird. Philomel and stormcock are out, common nightingale and mistle thrush are in. Going further afield, people in the US have been calling the red-breasted *Turdus migratorius* a robin for several hundred years while people in England have been calling a different bird by the same name for considerably longer without anyone being too worried about it. From now on the former is to be known as the American robin, to distinguish it from the (unfortunately unrelated, but you can't have everything) bird which has prior claim on the name, the European robin. Whether we can expect Americans to give up 'chickadee' and adopt the older English word – 'tit' – I am not so sure.

But what about the 60% or so of bird species not fortunate enough to live in an English-speaking country? Take, for example, the small sprightly greyish bird with white throat, a black band across its chest and a patch of chestnut brown on its forehead that goes by the scientific name of *Eremomela turneri* (a combination of the latinized forms of the Greek ερημομελα or 'desert songster' and the name of its European discoverer, the eccentric English naturalist and epicure Henry 'Mad Harry' Turner). What shall we call it – Turner's desert songster? The trouble with this is that although most members of the genus *Eremomela* are indeed found in deserts, this particular species is known only from rainforest. The chestnut-fronted black-banded white-throat? Getting a little clumsy, I think you will agree. When presented with birds of this type – and especially, for some reason, if they are small – those in charge of such matters usually settle for an anglicized version of the scientific name and leave it at that. *Cisticola hunteri* has thus become Hunter's cisticola; *Apalis ruddi* is known to all serious birdwatchers as Rudd's apalis; our little friend *Eremomela turneri* is now described in popular guides to the birds of East Africa as Turner's eremomela. And the only place where it is found, as you may remember George telling Harry Khan recently at the Nairobi Hilton, is Kakamega Forest in western Kenya.

'Did you see that ostrich again when we were taking off?'

Harry spooned the last piece of orange flesh from a slice of pawpaw. Now, should he go for the scrambled eggs or the poached?

'Ostrich?' said George. 'No. Anyway we've seen ostriches – right, Davo? Is there any bacon?'

'Behind the sausages.' The three of them were sitting at one of the tables on the veranda. 'What are they made of, do you think, Kenyan sausages?'

'I was once taken round a sausage factory in Toronto,' said Harry. 'Whatever's in these ones it can't be any worse. What's the plan?'

'The plan is . . . hang on a minute.' David put down his fork and grabbed his binoculars. 'Blimey O'Reilly. Look over there – George, Harry.'

'Where?' Harry pointed his own binoculars up into the dense tree canopy where something large was crashing about among the foliage. 'Oh yeah, I can see it.' He lowered the binoculars and rubbed his eyes. He raised them again. 'I can see it but I've never seen anything like it. What the hell is it?'

'That,' said David, consulting his guidebook, 'is *Corythaeola cristata*, your genuine large-as-life, one-and-only, great blue turaco.'

Ah yes, the great blue turaco. When the prizes are given out for the most unlikely bird, the great blue turaco will be lining up among the best of them. Take a chicken. Give it a large yellow beak with a red tip. Now give it a nice long tail. What colour shall we make it? A bit of red underneath perhaps, and its breast a nice apple green. We'll make most of the rest of it bright blue – blue head, blue neck, blue wings, blue back – though what about a bit more yellow under the tail and a smart black bar at the end? So far it's looking good but I can't help thinking there's something missing. I know. To set off that black band on the tail what we really need is a large black fan-shaped crest, right on the top of its head. There, what do you think? Is that an unlikely-looking bird or is that an unlikely-looking bird?

'It's wonderful,' said Harry.

'It's amazing,' said George.

'It's astounding,' said David, helping himself to some more bacon.

The turaco, which had settled down in full view at the end of a dead branch to preen its spectacular plumage, was now joined by another.

'Tok,' said the first bird.

'Tok. Tok. Tok,' said the second.

'Tok. Tok. Tok. Tok. Tok. Tok,' replied the first, which seemed to be some sort of turaco in-joke because both birds began a loud wheezy chuckle.

'That,' said Harry, 'is definitely one for the list.'

'Mmm,' said David. 'Hang on – what happened to all the sausages?'

Grey Parrot

33

At the club Mr Patel was transcribing the names of the birds that Harry Khan had seen that day. Though Turner's eremomela was notable on the list only by its absence (it is a very small bird, and it is rather drab) the Kakamega list was impressive. Below the great blue turaco were no fewer than twenty-six other new species, most of which the trio had spotted coming down to drink at the bird bath which the thoughtful and aviphilic guest-house owners had set up in the garden.

'Twenty-seven today,' said Patel with a smile. 'Pretty good going, Khan. That makes one hundred and ninety-nine in total.'

But on catching Mr Gopez's eye he turned down the corners of his mouth and raised his eyebrows in worried apprehension. Harry Khan was now more than sixty ahead. What chance did Malik have now? And where was Malik anyway?

The Tiger too had noticed the hands of the club clock were only minutes from the hour. A small knot of members were clustered around outside the main door scanning the entrance driveway.

Mr Malik had in fact left Benjamin's village in plenty of time to return to Nairobi by eight o'clock. It had taken them two and a half hours to get to the village. He calculated that if he left by four o'clock – no, make that three o'clock to allow for unforeseen hold-ups – he would make it to the club well before the evening count. But some hold-ups are more unforeseen than others – especially if they involve the use of one or more Kalashnikov AK47 assault rifles.

Of the approximately 70 million of these rugged and reliable firearms that have been manufactured since 1947 in a variety of locations, a not inconsiderable number have found their way to Kenya. No one knows exactly how many, for the guns are seldom in official hands but rather in the hands of criminals, bandits, gangsters, cattle rustlers and others of nefarious intent. Which is a pretty accurate job description of the two men who, as Mr Malik and Benjamin were driving away from the village and had almost reached the main highway, stepped out from behind a large advertising hoarding (remember Omo washes whiter?), AK47s cradled casually in their arms.

Two schools of opinion exist in Kenya on what to do when confronted by this kind of situation. Some say you should put your foot down and hope for the best. The other view is that you should on no account risk your life by so foolhardy an action. The correct thing to do is to stop, get out of the car with your hands up, and only then hope for the best. Mr Malik, you will remember from the recent incident in City Park, is of the latter persuasion. Under pretty much any imaginable conditions life is more important than property. Material things can be foregone or replaced. A life, once taken, cannot. On seeing the men with guns, this was Mr Malik's first thought. But even as he was thinking it a second thought occurred to him. If these men were to take his car he would never get back to the club in time for the count. If he did not get back in time he would lose the competition, and so lose the chance to take Rose Mbikwa – whose lovely voice that very morning had spoken his name on the telephone and still echoed in his ears – to the Hunt Club Ball. A third thought occurred to him. If he drove away it would not be just his life he would be risking. He had a passenger, and that passenger was not only an innocent boy but had just helped him see so many of the bird species of Kenya that he could still be in with a chance to take the woman of his dreams to the Hunt Club Ball. The thoughts were not sequential but simultaneous, as was his decision. He must stop the car. At that moment his passenger spoke.

'Go, Mr Malik! Go!'

And his right foot, which had been about to move from the accelerator pedal to the brake, slammed down hard. The car was in second gear. The rear wheels, instead of powering the car forward, lost their grip on the dry dusty road and started to spin. Mr Malik had but a glimpse of the startled faces of the men with guns before he and they were enveloped in a thick cloud of dust.

'Go, Mr Malik! Go!'

Mr Malik was still trying to go. He took his foot off the throttle just enough to feel one of the tyres grip an exposed rock. The car stopped sliding to the left and jerked forward. Careful to accelerate more gently this time, Mr Malik pointed it towards where he hoped the road would be. As he emerged from the cloud of brown dust he found his judgement had been correct. Faster and faster he drove, changing up into third gear then fourth, away from the billboard, the dust and its sinister occupants. But not fast enough. He didn't hear the crack of the first 7.62mm round as it left the gun, but he heard the smack of it piercing his rear window and hitting the dashboard, right between him and Benjamin. He didn't hear the second round being fired either, but he heard the bang of a bursting tyre and felt the back of the Mercedes drop. How far can you drive an old green Mercedes 450 SEL on a burst tyre? Now was the time to find out.

I have mentioned that ever since 1947, when Mikhail Kalashnikov designed the AK47, this semi-automatic rifle has been popular for its reliability and ruggedness. These are qualities that come at a price. One reason that the mechanism of the AK47 does not get easily fouled with mud, water or pale brown dust is that there are relatively generous clearances between its various moving parts. These same clearances also mean that its accuracy is not all it might be. Beyond about a hundred metres, hitting your target becomes as much a matter of luck as skill. The two bandits knew this. Puncturing the car's tyre had been one such lucky shot. Thanks to that lucky shot the car and its passengers would not get far and there was no use wasting ammunition. I should further point out here something that Benjamin suspected but Mr Malik did not. These men were not after Mr Malik, nor his wallet or his car. They were not local men, they were not even Samburu or Turkana come down from the wild north. Benjamin had immediately recognized them as Somalis. And though there is a long history of Somali tribesmen raiding far into Kenya for cattle, these modern raiders had other booty in mind – human booty. In Somalia, as in neighbouring Chad and parts of Ethiopia, a very good price can be had for a fit young man to sell as a soldier. Benjamin did not want to be a soldier.

'Go, Mr Malik! Go!'

The old Mercedes rattled and bumped along for about two hundred metres until the blown tyre broke free from the rim. Mr Malik saw its shredded remains in the wing mirror, and still he drove on. He had the idea that if Benjamin could move over to the opposite corner it would somehow balance the car back on to three wheels. The trouble was it had been the rear left tyre that had been shot and the opposite corner was occupied by the driver's seat, which he was himself sitting in.

'Benjamin,' he yelled above the rattles and shakes. 'Can you climb on to my lap?'

Without questioning, Benjamin wriggled across. The car did not tip up on to three wheels as Mr Malik had hoped, but the manoeuvre should take a little weight off the damaged wheel. Now he had to decide how far he could drive on a bare wheel rim without doing permanent damage either to wheel or axle. If he could get far enough from the gunmen to give him time to stop and fit the spare they still had a chance. Except that he had never changed a car wheel in his life.

'Have you ever changed a wheel, Benjamin?'

'Only on a bicycle, sir. But on a bus I have seen it done.'

The back wheel was sounding worse and worse.

'We'll have to try it. If I can get round the corner then they won't be able to see us. With luck they won't realize that we've stopped.'

As soon as the gunmen were out of sight of his rear-view mirror Mr Malik eased off the throttle, changed down and gently braked.

'Come,' he said, opening the door. 'We need to find the spare wheel, and that thing – the thing that lifts the car.'

'Jack?'

Mr Malik winced.

'Yes, that's it. Somewhere in the back, I think.'

Benjamin scuttled round to the back of the car where the boot was already open.

'Can you see it? That thing, and the wheel?'

Benjamin found the spare wheel beneath a flap at the bottom of the luggage space. Jack there was none.

'It's no use, Mr Malik. They will be here soon. You must come, sir. Come with me.'

'But . . . where to? What do you mean, come?'

'Come, sir. I will hide you, then I will go to get help.'

Benjamin was right. There was no point in waiting for the Somalis to arrive. Though Mr Malik hadn't seen a vehicle and supposed the men must be on foot, they couldn't be more than five minutes behind. Benjamin began scrambling up the hillside.

'This way, sir. There is a hole. You will hide there while I go and get help.'

'Get help – where?'

'At my school, sir. It is just over the hill here. It is a very good school.'

Mr Malik had no alternative but to follow him up the hill to a small cave, just large enough for him to crawl inside.

'Wait here, sir. Do not come out until I come back.'

Sandgrouse

34

The clock at the Asadi Club ticked towards eight. Where was Mr Malik? Where was the list of birds he had seen that day? The crowd on the steps outside was joined by Mr Patel, Mr Gopez and Tiger Singh. Surely Malik would not let them down, surely he would not tarnish the honour of the club? A strange sound was heard, sounding first like the growl of a distant lion, then the thunder of a thousand hoofbeats on the hard dry plains. As it grew nearer the sound resolved itself into the painful crunch and graunch of a car that has not only lost most of its exhaust system but whose rear axle is damaged beyond any hope of repair. Mr Malik's green Mercedes limped into the car park just as the clock began to chime eight. There was not a man in the Asadi Club – no matter who his money was on – who was not cheering Mr Malik's arrival. Not least among them was Mr Patel. He bounded down the steps and flung open the car door.

'Malik, just in time. What happened to your car? It looks as though a rock's fallen on it. Oh, never mind. Come on in. Have you got your list?'

Mr Malik reached into the back of the car for his notebook and thrust it into the hands of Mr Patel.

'Here, count those. And would someone please get a drink for my friend – my guest – here. Coca-Cola, I think – a large one.'

Benjamin, sitting in the front passenger seat, grinned.

'I say, old chap,' said the Tiger, shouting to make himself heard over the hubbub, 'is that a bullet hole in the back window?'

'Getting desperate, eh Malik?' said Mr Gopez. 'Been taking potshots at the little blighters. Against the rules, you know.'

'I'll tell you all about it later. Right now, I need to wash.'

Shampooed and showered, and with clothes which a good brushing had made not exactly spotless but certainly more respectable, Mr Malik appeared at the bar to renewed cheering. Even Harry Khan was cheering.

'Wouldn't want to win by a scratching.'

While Patel rechecked his score and tallied up the total, Mr Malik told them of his day's adventures. First he told them about the birds. Benjamin had been right about seeing more birds in his village than in Nairobi. It was not only an oasis for humans and their livestock in the parched landscape, it was an oasis for birds. At a little puddle near where the old people lived, he and Mr Malik seemed to have seen all the birds of the desert. They were mostly small birds, birds that eke out a living from the seeds and insects of the dry country, but a species is a species no matter how diminutive its representatives. Various finches, waxbills, pipits and wagtails were the commonest, but there were starlings and weavers too. Doves were frequent visitors to the puddle – tiny Namaqua doves, larger laughing doves and small flocks of ring-necked doves – and although not a single great blue turaco had put in an appearance a gang of their close relatives, go-away birds, arrived at one point bleating their strange cries. In the early afternoon a sandgrouse flew down, which according to Benjamin was unusual as these birds normally appeared only early in the morning. From the black patch around its beak and its white eyebrow Mr Malik was able to identify it as a black-faced sandgrouse. They watched enthralled as the bird waded into the puddle, fluffed out its feathers and squatted as low as it could go.

'I have often seen them do this, but only the fathers,' said Benjamin, and Mr Malik, though he had never seen a sandgrouse before, remembered something Rose Mbikwa had once said on the Tuesday morning bird walk.

'It is for their chicks,' he said. 'They take water back to the nest for their chicks to drink. They have special feathers underneath, you see, like a sponge.'

Benjamin was impressed, both with the bird's behaviour and with Mr Malik's knowledge.

Perched in trees and bushes at varying distances around the puddle were several kinds of shrikes and hawks. A female shikra, the smallest African sparrowhawk, never seemed to leave its thorn tree while a larger hawk, the pale chanting goshawk, made frequent flyovers on the lookout for unwary prey. In all, according to Mr Patel's calculations, Mr Malik had seen sixty-two new species that day.

'Yes, yes,' said Mr Gopez, 'but never mind about the birds, what happened to your car?'

'Ah, the car.'

So Mr Malik told them all about the two Somalis and the AK47s and the missing thing, and what had happened then.

From the shadows of the cave Mr Malik could see his stranded car on the road below. All was quiet. Not a cricket chirped, not a bird sang. After what seemed like an hour but Mr Malik knew from his watch was no more than fifteen minutes, around the corner came the two bandits. They were laughing and joking with each other, confident in the knowledge that their quarry wouldn't get far and that they and their guns were a match for an old man and a boy. After checking the car they laughed again. They must have seen that though the spare tyre had been taken out, there was no jack. One of them spoke a few incomprehensible words and they split

170

up. It was clear they were going to search the area. How long would it be until they found him? They had not gone more than a few steps when one of the men shouted to the other and pointed up the hill towards him. They had seen him. All was lost.

But then Mr Malik heard the crack of a gun and a rumbling sound. From the slopes above him came a large rock, followed down the hill by another, then more. The rocks bounced and tumbled past the entrance to his cave, smashing down on to the road below him. One of the bandits raised his gun only to find it knocked from his grasp by a flying boulder. Another gunshot came from the hill above, followed by a barrage of blood-curdling whoops. To Mr Malik's astonishment the two gunmen took one more look, then fled.

'Sir. Mr Malik, sir. Are you there?'

Mr Malik had never in his life been so glad to see the boy. He crawled from the cave and looked around for the armed posse that Benjamin seemed somehow to have summoned from nowhere. What he saw was Benjamin surrounded by a group of about fifty children. Behind them, grinning widely and wielding what appeared to be a starting pistol, stood an older man.

'Mr Malik, sir, this is my teacher, Mr Haputale, and these are my cousins and nephews and nieces and friends from the school. They have come to help us.'

The children giggled, the schoolmaster gravely shook Mr Malik's hand. Benjamin directed a dozen or so of the bigger children down to the car.

'Now my friends, when I say lift, lift.'

In no time at all the wheel was changed and they were on their way.

'Benjamin,' said Mr Malik as, to waves from the children and the schoolmaster, they headed down the road towards Nairobi, 'Benjamin, you are quite right. It is a very good school.'

Nightjar

35

'My dear fellow,' said Mr Gopez draining the last drops from his glass, 'do you really expect us to believe that not only did you see – how many did you say, Patel, sixty-two? – new birds, but you found time to fight off a bunch of bandits?'

'Yeah,' said Harry Khan. 'Are you sure you didn't just get a flat on the Uhuru Road?'

'Mr Gopez,' said the Tiger. 'Are you questioning the word of a member of the Asadi Club?'

'Not at all, Tiger, not at all. Just wondering, that's all.'

'Good.'

And Mr Malik suddenly remembered.

'There is another matter I must raise before the Committee. I apologize for not doing it sooner.'

He cleared his throat.

'I have not yet told you how I got my car back. This morning I spoke to Mrs Mbikwa on the telephone. It was she who told me where to find it.'

There was a short silence.

'Hey,' said Harry Khan. 'No contact, right? Sounds like contact to me. Looks like you might be in a bit of trouble here, Jack.'

Tiger Singh looked from one to the other, took from his briefcase the printed sheets containing the rules of the competition and began reading.

'"Both parties also agree that between now and the moment when the Wager is settled, neither will initiate contact – personal, telephonic or epistolary, nor through any third person nor by any other means – with the aforementioned lady." Is this what is concerning you, Malik?'

'Yes,' said Mr Malik. 'It was inadvertent on my part, but this morning I was undoubtedly in telephonic contact with Mrs Mbikwa.'

'But my dear chap you've already told us that *she* phoned *you*. Ergo you did not *intitiate* contact, ergo you have – as I'm sure my learned friends will agree – no case to answer.'

His friends nodded their assent. Harry Khan frowned. Mr Malik gave a sigh of relief.

'But,' continued the Tiger, 'I think there may be a graver matter for our consideration. Mr Khan, I have been thinking. Did I hear you correctly earlier saying something about a bird bath?'

'Yeah, at the guest house. There's a bird bath set up right next to the veranda.'

'A bird bath – are you sure?'

'Yeah. You know, with water. The birds come down to drink there.'

'Then, gentlemen, I feel I should call your attention to Rule Five.'

'Rule Five?' said Harry Khan.

'Rule Five?' said Mr Malik.

'Rule Five, gentlemen. Which clearly states that the use of bait, lures, tethered birds or pre-recorded sound to attract birds is strictly forbidden. I'm afraid that if a bird bath full of water isn't bait, I don't know what is.'

A hush descended on the bar.

'I think that you may well have a point, Tiger,' said Mr Patel.

Mr Malik said nothing. Yes, the Tiger did have a point, but it was a point that might not only apply to Harry Khan.

'If the Committee will allow me, I would like to interject here,' he said. 'If the birds that Mr Khan saw today are to be ruled out, then I think mine must be too.'

'What?' said Mr Gopez. 'Why? How?'

And so Mr Malik explained again how he had driven with Benjamin down on to the plains, where it was dry as dry could be. But that the little village they went to was like an oasis.

'Why? Because of a spring. Water is pumped from the spring into a large tank, and pipes take the water to the houses and to the fields.'

'But what on earth's that got to do with bird baths?'

'Because, A.B., one of the pipes has a small leak, just near where the old people live. But nobody minds about this leak because the puddle that collects there is where the birds come to drink. In the dry times the people like to know that the birds have somewhere to drink.'

'So you're saying . . . ?'

'That it is just like the bird bath at the guest house. It is there for the birds, but not to attract the birds, if you see what I mean. Just like the bird bath. They are the same.'

The Tiger looked round at his two fellow Committee members.

'Gentlemen, shall we discuss this further?'

'I don't think there is any need,' said Mr Gopez.

'If it's all right with you two, and with Malik and Khan, of course,' said Mr Patel, 'it's all right with me.'

'In that case,' said the Tiger, 'any objections are overruled. Mr Patel, will you please double-check the scores.'

'Khan, one hundred and ninety-nine. Malik, one hundred and ninety-eight.'

'Whoa,' said Harry. 'Getting close.'

'And I need hardly remind you, gentlemen, that tomorrow is the last day. I look forward to seeing you both back here at the club at noon for the final tally. Now if you will excuse me, I have promised to take my wife to the Bar Association dinner.'

'I'd better be going too, guys,' said Harry. 'It looks like I'm going to need an early start.'

'And please excuse me too,' said Mr Malik. 'It has been a tiring day.'

'Good night, Tiger. Night, Khan,' said Mr Gopez. He turned to Mr Malik and lowered his voice. 'Now they've gone, Malik old chap, tell us. What really happened to your car?'

Kenyan Crested
Guineafowl

36

'You would have thought,' said Harry Khan, brushing away a mosquito, 'that people had better things to do on a Friday night.'

'Saturday morning, actually, Harry,' said David, swatting at another with half-hearted hand.

'Bloody oath, Davo,' said George, sitting down beside them on the hard wood bench. 'Friday, Saturday, what's the difference?'

Outside a hadada called from a nearby fever tree. A guineafowl gave its weird, loud cry. Through the thick iron bars of their cell they watched a pink dawn breaking.

There are, as all keen students of African ornithology are aware, four species of guineafowl native to Kenya. Though they all sound much the same they can be distinguished by slight differences in size and plumage. The commonest is the helmeted guineafowl, whose distinctive dark grey, white-spotted shapes are often seen in small groups in the drier parts of the country. Less common are the vulturine and common crested guineafowl, while rarest of all is the Kenyan crested guineafowl – now found only in the Sokoke Forest just north of Mombasa (should you ever be lucky enough to see one you will be able to recognize it by the bluish tinge to its spots and a little more red around the eye). Coming as he did from the coast at Takaungu, this last species was the one with which Private William Hakara was most familiar and of which he was most fond. Roast, fried or stewed, there was nothing William Hakara liked more than a fine fresh guineafowl, and from childhood he had developed considerable skill in obtaining them.

Kenyan crested guineafowl are shy and wary birds. They stick to one patch of forest, where they know every twig and track. It is next to impossible to creep up on one to shoot or grab it. But they possess great curiosity, and nothing incites their curiosity more than the colour blue. I have never seen this for myself but I am assured by my friend Kennedy that he has watched a Kenyan crested guineafowl staring at an empty pack of Clear Sky cigarettes for minutes at a time. Should you want to trap one of these birds, therefore, the best bait to use is not grain or fruit or anything that the bird might eat, but simply something blue. As a child, William Hakara always used small pieces of blue cloth which he would tie to a stick, the stick forming the trigger for a simple spring trap – bird pecks cloth, stick releases branch, branch pulls noose, noose catches bird. Often he would set a trap on the way to school and the resulting catch would be ready for him to pick up on the way home.

On leaving school William Hakara had been delighted to be accepted into the army, though disappointed when after basic training he had been posted not back to the coast (as he had hoped) but to Nairobi and the headquarters of the 1st/2nd Battalion Kenyan Rifle Brigade. So imagine his delight that first week when on evening patrol inside the perimeter fence he had heard a familiar soft clucking coming from some bushes just the other side. The next evening he carried with him on patrol not only his rifle but a pair of pliers, a length of fishing line and a scrap of blue cloth. No one would notice the small hole in the back fence right at ground level, just big enough for a curious bird. With luck, no one would notice the cloth tied to a stick, or the branch bent over with its noose of fishing line. And with even more luck the very next night after perimeter patrol he would be sucking the bones of a fine roast guineafowl.

His first thought when he saw flashlights near the fence was that someone was trying to steal his dinner. But if so they were making rather a noisy job of it. His second thought was that some of his fellow soldiers were coming home late and drunk from the Blue Beat Hotel and Bar on Magadi Road, trying to hop over the back fence into the barracks to avoid the MPs, and perhaps he should help them. But again, they seemed to be making a hell of a racket doing so. It was only when he crept closer to the fence and saw three men with torches and binoculars that he arrived at his third thought. These men were neither trap robbers nor fellow soldiers. They were intruders.

'Halt,' he said. 'Who goes there?'

On the other side of the fence Harry Khan thought he had seen something move – a bird perhaps?

'Shhh,' he said. 'Keep it quiet, David – you'll frighten the owls.'

'That wasn't me. I'm right here behind you.'

'Then stop playing around, George.'

'It wasn't me either.'

'Halt,' said the voice again, 'or I fire.'

Fire? Harry looked around. There was David with his spotlight, there was George with his. And there, over by the fence, was another light. He did some quick thinking. The Modern East African Tourist Inn was long closed, his red Mercedes the only vehicle in the car park. They had not seen lights from any other cars drive up. It was dark. They were alone, unarmed, and far from help.

'George, David – halting OK with you?'

As they halted the voice spoke again.

'Good. Now turn off your torches and put them down on the ground. Please. And put your hands up in the air.'

Three 600,000 candle power spotlights were gently lowered to the ground. Three pairs of hands were raised. They heard what sounded like the click and crackle of a radio and a minute later a vehicle rounded the fence and pulled up behind them.

Other lights shone bright, and glinting in their beams was the barrel of a gun.

'Shit,' said Harry under his breath. Then, 'Who are you, what do you want?'

'I think we will be the ones asking the questions, gentlemen,' said another voice. 'Turn. March.'

And turn and march they did – past the jeep, past the parked Mercedes, past the entrance to the MEATI, along the road and towards some gates whose large sign identified them as the entrance to the Headquarters of the 1st/2nd Battalion Kenyan Rifle Brigade.

Owlet

37

Little shocks a lawyer. The things men do and the reasons they do them, the lengths to which men go to conceal what they have done and to hide their deepest fears and desires and emotions – even from themselves – all these are seldom hidden from the lawyer's forensic gaze. H. H. Singh, LLB, MA (Oxon.) nonetheless had to confess to his wife mild surprise at the telephone call he received that Saturday morning just as he was about to leave for the club. It was from Colonel Jomo Bukoto. One of his men had arrested some intruders at the barracks and one of these intruders had been asking for him. Harry Khan – did he know the man?

The Tiger made a couple of phone calls, changed his clothes and arrived at the barracks just thirty-five minutes after he had taken the call. After giving his name to the guard at the gate he was escorted to the officers' mess where he found Colonel Bukoto, in golfing attire, about to crack a boiled egg. Beside his egg was a plate of buttered toast, already cut up into soldiers. Standing beside him was a larger soldier dressed in lieutenant's uniform.

'Good of you to see me, Colonel.'

Colonel Bukoto turned and looked him up and down – and now you will see what a fine lawyer Tiger Singh really is. For the Tiger was dressed in the pale slacks, short-sleeved shirt, sleeveless jumper and loafers that immediately identified him as a fellow golfer.

'Mr Singh, I take it.' The colonel smiled. 'Sit down, old fellow. Tea?'

Though time was of the essence the business must not be hurried.

'Thank you, Colonel.' The Tiger made to sit down, hesitated, felt in his back pocket and removed a yellow plastic golf tee then settled on to the chair. 'Tea would be lovely.'

'So,' said the colonel, signalling to an orderly, 'this man Khan.'

'Ah yes, Colonel Bukoto. Harry Khan. Perhaps you could fill me in on some of the details?'

'Found by one of our guards late last night outside the back fence, trying to break in apparently.'

'Alone?'

'No. With a couple of *wazungu* – Australian. They say they're birdwatchers.'

'Ah.' The Tiger paused to accept the cup of tea. 'Do you believe them?'

'I don't know.'

'Birdwatchers, you say?'

The tone was flat, but the way the Tiger's brow creased slightly as he spoke the words made the colonel, who had once been a fan of the works of Ian Fleming, sure he remembered something about birdwatchers in one of them. *The Man with the Golden Gun*?

'You mean . . . ?'

'Tell me, Colonel, has either of these other chaps asked you to contact the Australian High Commission?'

'Yes, they both have.'

'Hmmm,' said the Tiger.

'Khan has been asking for you, though.'

'It's not Khan I'm worried about, Colonel. I know him. Playboy type. Pots of money, not a bad handicap. Matter of fact I'm supposed to be teamed up with him in the club final this afternoon – I don't know if he mentioned it? But the other two . . .' The Tiger leaned forward in his chair. 'They've asked for the High Commissioner, you say?'

'Yes.'

'I see.'

'And some mosquito repellant.'

'Ah. Did you give them any?'

'No.'

The Tiger nodded.

'If I may say so, Colonel, you clearly know your stuff. Tell me, have they been separated yet?'

Colonel Bukoto turned to his ADC.

'Have they been separated yet?'

'No, sir. You didn't . . .'

'Do it. At once.'

The ADC barked out an order to another uniformed soldier who bustled away.

'Have you talked to them yourself, Colonel?'

'No, not yet. I thought it best to leave it a little while.'

'Of course.' The Tiger picked up his cup and took a sip of the hot tea. 'I don't have much experience of this kind of thing but as far as the legal side of things goes I imagine you're on pretty solid ground here.'

'Yes – I checked, of course.'

The colonel nodded to his ADC.

'Statutory power of arrest within two hundred metres of any military installation, sir. Power of detention and interrogation for twenty-four hours, sir.'

'And that,' said the colonel, picking up his napkin and wiping the toast crumbs from his moustache, 'is even without the new anti-terrorism legislation.'

'That gives you plenty of time to question them, then. Time for nine holes before you even start, I'd say.' The Tiger smiled, then frowned. 'Oh Colonel, if it's all right with you I'd better see Khan, but would you mind if I just phoned the club first?'

The Tiger had tried his best to persuade the colonel.

'No, Mr Singh, I'm afraid I must insist.'

'But there are rules, regulations.'

'Mr Singh, if I may say so I make the rules around here.'

'But . . .'

'No, my mind is made up. You take him. I'll get the story out of the other two, don't you worry about that.'

'But Colonel, surely this is highly irregular? I mean, the chap's under lawful detention and all that.'

'Well, he can be lawfully undetended then, can't he? Leave it to me.'

'But really, it's only the club comp. There'll be another chance, next year or . . .'

The colonel held up a hand.

'Mr Singh, consider it an order.'

And so on the last Saturday of the bird competition we find Tiger Singh, still in his golfing attire, arriving at the Asadi Club with fifteen minutes to spare and with an unusually subdued Harry Khan in tow behind him. Harry has not, of course, added a single species to his list. His plans of night spotting, followed by a few fruitful hours birdwatching in Nairobi National Park before noon have, thanks to Private William Hakara, come to nought.

But what of Mr Malik?

Greenbul

38

Beneath his mosquito net at Number 12 Garden Lane Mr Malik had also spent a sleepless night. Yesterday's experience out looking for birds in Benjamin's village seemed to have put things in new perspective. He had never been so close to death. Life seemed different. Today, he would not be looking for birds. As soon as he had drunk his morning Nescafé and eaten his two breakfast bananas he telephoned for a taxi. He directed the driver along Garden Lane to the roundabout. Taking the second exit they drove past the telephone exchange and post office, turned right at the mosque and at 8.30 a.m. precisely pulled up outside the Aga Khan Hospital. Had he not already missed one visit due to this bird thing, this Harry Khan thing? No, there were more important matters, more important even than winning a chance to take Rose Mbikwa to the Hunt Club Ball.

For the next two hours, as he had on so many Saturday mornings for the last four years, Mr Malik sat by the bedside of the sick and dying, talking with them or not talking but always listening, and always thinking. And afterwards he had gone (without his new binoculars) to the old cemetery with its broken wall and memories, to think some more. Yes, there were more important things. Do birds, he wondered as he watched the scrawny chickens pecking round the gravestones, mourn their dead? Do birds have regrets?

When Mr Malik arrived at the Asadi Club at ten minutes to twelve that morning he found it so crowded he could hardly squeeze through the doorway into the bar.

'Malik, is that you?' shouted Mr Gopez.

'I think you're a winner, old boy,' said Patel.

Harry Khan had already revealed to the Committee that he had seen no new species since the night before, and the sorry tale behind it. He was still one ahead, but surely Malik had seen something.

'Give the man space,' said the Tiger. 'Now, Malik, tell us what you've seen since yesterday.'

'Oh, nothing new,' said Mr Malik, 'nothing at all.'

'Yes yes yes,' said Mr Gopez, 'but how many *birds* have you seen?'

'None.'

The bar went silent.

'Gentlemen,' said the Tiger, his voice raised. 'We have already learned something of Khan's unfortunate experience and that since last night he has seen no new birds to add to his total. Malik, are you now saying that you too have no additions to make to your list?'

Mr Malik nodded.

The bar erupted into cheers and hoots and catcalls. Harry Khan's face changed from one of resigned despondency to the broadest of grins. It was with some difficulty that the Tiger ushered Mr Malik to the table in the corner of the room where the rest of the Committee had found seats.

'My God, Malik,' said Mr Gopez, 'surely you must have seen one bally bird. Where on earth have you been all morning?'

Mr Malik, thinking of the people he had visited in the hospital, then the hour he had spent in the old cemetery, smiled.

'I fear that the only birds I have seen today, my dear friends, are a few old hens.'

Mr Gopez dropped his face in his hands. Mr Patel gave a slow shake of his head. The Tiger said nothing, but then he spoke.

'Then I think, gentlemen,' he said in his softest voice, 'that we have a draw.'

Mr Gopez raised his head.

'Draw? What – the chickens, you mean? Yes, Tiger. Most amusing. Very bloody funny.'

'Chickens,' mused Mr Patel. 'Hmm.'

'Indeed the chickens,' said Tiger Singh. 'Nothing in the rules, as far as I am aware, rules out a chicken.'

'But it's a domestic bird,' said Mr Gopez. 'It's not even native to bloody Africa.'

'As I say, nothing in the rules excludes domestic species, and nothing excludes species that have been introduced.'

'But a chicken . . . ?' said Mr Malik.

The clock struck twelve.

It took the Committee nearly an hour of debate and a most thorough reinspection of the rules before they made their final judgement. The chicken, though domesticated, was unconfined and unrestrained and was ruled an eligible bird. Mr Malik had informed them of seeing it before the deadline expired. It must be added to his list. The result was therefore a draw.

'So,' said Mr Gopez, ' what do we do now?'

'I'll tell you what you do,' said a voice from the bar. 'Toss for it.'

The voice (which you will not be surprised to hear belonged to Sanjay Bashu) was echoed by a score of others, several of whom were only too happy to provide a coin. Amidst the shower of shillings Harry Khan raised his voice.

'If it's OK with Jack, it's OK with me.'

Mr Malik was thinking that it was probably not OK with Jack when another member spoke.

'Hang on. I didn't put up five lakh to be won or lost on the toss of a coin. If it's a draw, bets are off.'

The crowd now seemed evenly divided between those calling for the toss and those who wanted the wager cancelled. It was again the Tiger's turn to speak up.

'Gentlemen, gentlemen. May I remind you of the circumstances surrounding the initiation of this wager, this competition? The true prize, you may remember, is not a monetary one. It is for the hand, be it temporary, of a lady. And I think you will all agree that such a matter is most unsuitable – monstrously unsuitable it might be said – to be settled with the toss of a coin. No, gentlemen, a draw is a draw. In this instance I think we will have to agree that all bets are cancelled.'

Which was a relief to Mr Malik, who had been thinking along much the same lines himself.

'Thanks, Tiger,' he said.

'Well, all right and all very well,' said Mr Gopez. 'But that still doesn't solve the problem.'

'Problem, A.B.?' said Mr Patel.

'Yes, what about the invitation business? I mean what now – the bet is cancelled but they are both going to ask her, is it?'

'I see what you mean, A.B. Just the problem we were trying to avoid. Putting the lady in an invidious position and all that.'

'I've been thinking about it too,' said Mr Malik.

The three members of the Committee turned their faces towards him.

'I've been thinking about it, and have decided that in the circumstances it is only right . . .' Mr Malik saw Harry Khan appear through the crowd. He raised his voice. 'That as a senior member of the Asadi Club, and in the present circumstances, it is right and proper for me to withdraw from the competition. I shall not ask Mrs Rose Mbikwa to the ball.'

A moment's silence was followed by a general gasp from the room.

'Are you sure about that, old chap?' said Mr Patel.

'Perhaps we should talk it over,' said Mr Gopez. 'Don't want to rush these things, not after all you've gone through.'

'No, exactly,' said the Tiger. 'It would be fairer if neither of you ask her.'

'My mind,' said Mr Malik, 'is made up.'

Yes, he thought, there were more important things.

Harry Khan smiled. The Tiger stood up and turned towards him.

'In that case, Mr Khan, it looks as though you have won. There seems to be no reason against, nor impediment to, your asking Mrs Mbikwa to the Nairobi Hunt Club Ball.'

'Thanks, Tiger. And thanks, guys – you too, Jack. It's been fun, real fun.'

His white smile broadened further.

'Now, where's that telephone? Looks like this could be some little lady's lucky day.'

Whimbrel

39

'Well,' said Mr Patel as the three members of the now disbanded Special Committee sat down that evening around their usual table at the club, 'who'd have thought it?'

Mr Gopez shook his head.

'What on earth made him do it?' he said. 'I know he didn't win, but he didn't actually lose.'

'I must admit I was myself surprised by Malik's action – his *abdication* if I may so put it,' said the Tiger. 'As was my wife when I told her.'

'I can't help wondering if those bandits had anything to do with it.'

'Took the wind out of his dhoti, you mean?' said Mr Gopez.

'Maybe he actually felt sorry for poor old Khan.'

'All that business at the barracks, you mean?' said Mr Patel. 'Yes, Tiger. You haven't told us yet what happened.'

'*Sub judice*, I'm afraid.'

'Oh come on, Tiger,' said Mr Gopez. 'You can tell us, can't you?'

The Tiger thought for a moment.

'I suppose there is no harm in recounting the facts of the case. It appears that late last night Harry Khan was discovered by an army chap snooping round the barracks, the ones on Limuru Road.'

'Down by the MEATI, you mean?'

'The very same.'

'What on earth was he doing there?'

'According to what he told me, he and two associates – a couple of Australian tourists he'd teamed up with – were attempting to chalk up a few new species by torchlight. Nothing in the rules against it, I suppose.'

Mr Gopez grunted.

'Damned silly place to go flashing torches around.'

'Quite so, A.B., though I imagine all three parties were unaware of this at the time. However, the army – and Colonel Jomo Bukoto of the 1st/2nd Battalion Kenyan Rifle Brigade in particular – takes a dim view of such activities.'

'So how on earth did you spring them?'

'I regret it was not *them*, A.B. – only *him*. And that is one of the matters which will have to remain confidential.'

Mr Gopez grunted an unwilling assent.

'So the other two chaps, you mean they're still in the clink?'

The Tiger consulted his wristwatch.

'I would imagine that the colonel may have finished his round of golf by now and may be interviewing them as we speak. Tricky business, but I doubt whether it will go to court – probably just a quiet little deportation.'

'Deportation? But aren't they innocent?'

'Innocent in intent, perhaps, A.B., but not in deed. There are laws against creeping round military installations at night, even if you are just looking for birds.'

'But won't the Australians put up a fuss?' said Mr Patel.

'It's quite possible that their High Commissioner may have something to say but it is a tricky situation. While our government is ever anxious to make everything tickety-boo for tourists, it is equally keen at the moment to show that we are up to the mark as far as security goes. My guess is that the security issue will be the winner.'

'How long do you think they've got then, these two chaps, before they're bundled out?'

'That, I think, depends on how much publicity the government wants.'

A. B. Gopez gave a large sniff.

'They'll milk this one for all it's worth – mark my words. Headlines for months, I shouldn't wonder.'

Mr Patel turned to his friend with an innocent smile. 'Oh,' he said, reaching for his wallet. 'I don't know.'

Like every one of the 1,431,116 women who according to the most recent census officially inhabit the city of Nairobi (and probably twice that number who live there unofficially), Rose Mbikwa was unaware of these events. Since returning from Switzerland after her operation, her main concern had simply been to get well soon. Her surgeon had assured her that although she had an excellent chance of making a full recovery it was not advisable – indeed might be counterproductive – to hurry these things. Her vision was already much improved by the new artificial lens but the eye itself would take time to recover. She should rest it, and continue to wear the eyepatch out of doors for at least a month.

As she made her way down the stairs from the bedroom a week after her return to Nairobi, Rose was in a reflective mood. She had been disappointed, she realized, that she had not seen Mr Malik when he came to pick up his car. Why she felt so, she could not quite put a finger on. With his funny comb-over and shy manner he was a strange man but she knew that he was a good man, and it is goodness that counts. He had been coming on the bird walks for a long time now, and he always made sure that old Mercedes of his was filled with young students before they went anywhere. And he always made sure to call everyone's attention if he saw something they might like to see – but modestly, not like some. Perhaps it was also something to do with that AIDS Aware sticker. She had one just like it on her own car. Perhaps it was all of these things. And she knew that, like her, he loved Kenya and the birds of Kenya.

Rose was also slightly disappointed – though in a different way – that Harry Khan wasn't in town. Harry was fun, and while she was away she had been thinking that it was time to have more fun in her life. A little less of the past, a little less of the future, a little more of the present. Harry had left a message to say he'd be away from Nairobi for a week or so on business – something to do with franchises. Maybe they could get together when he got back? Yes, maybe they would. But perhaps another cause of Rose's disappointment, though, was that when you arrive back from some time away – even if it is only nine days – it feels good to know that everyone is pleased to see you back, or at least has noticed your absence. She should drop by the museum later. Though she had taken in advance a whole month's leave, there might be some cheques to sign or urgent letters to see to. Under its piratical patch her eye was still a little sore, but otherwise she was feeling fine. In fact, she might take a little walk, right now.

I have mentioned before that a feature of Nairobi is its rubbish disposal system. The smoky bonfires that help keep its streets relatively clean by consuming anything from dead leaves to dead dogs (this is true, I have seen it with my own eyes) do so at the expense of the air above. Combined with the smoke of fifty thousand badly tuned diesel engines, they make for a distinctive urban aroma. Yet on that October day the smell that greeted Rose's nose as she walked down the driveway of her house towards the gate was almost delicious in its familiarity.

Those cars, though. There were more than ever on the street outside the house next door. She really would have to have a word with the judge. How Mr Malik's old Mercedes had ended up among them would presumably remain a mystery – perhaps the thieves had just been looking for a place to dump it where it wouldn't be noticed for a while. But she was glad she had recognized the car and even more glad that Mr Malik had got it back. And she *would* speak to the judge, but she wouldn't do it yet. With a cheerful nod to her number one askari, old Mukhisa, she adjusted her eyepatch and set off along Serengeti Gardens. She walked away from the parked cars with hardly a glance at the small bonfire in the gutter outside the judge's house, and off down the hill. But then the rain started, heavy rain. Rose, having taken no umbrella, decided to turn around. Never mind, she had plenty to do inside. For one thing, there was that invitation which had just arrived. She must send a reply. Head down, she hurried back to the house.

Can you worry both more and less about the same thing at the same time? It certainly seemed that way to Mr Malik. No, not about losing his chance to ask Rose Mbikwa to the ball – that business was over and done with and so were his chances, even though the tickets to the ball had come at last and were now lying on the table by the front door. He would decide what to do with them later. And his car was back from the repairers with the rear axle and rear window replaced and the roof beaten back into a rough approximation of its original shape. But there was still the missing notebook.

On the one hand the fact he had not heard anything probably meant that it had been lost or forgotten or thrown away. But Mr Malik couldn't stop the niggling thought that the very same fact might mean that even now it was being examined by someone who he'd rather was not examining it. Someone in the government, or the judiciary. How they would love to know the identity of that thorn in their sides, Dadukwa. What they would do if they found out.

'Daddy,' said his daughter Petula as she joined him on the veranda one morning and noticed that once again he had eaten only one of his breakfast bananas, 'is anything the matter?'

He had been very quiet of late and looking a little grey. He hadn't been to the club all week. She hoped it wasn't anything to do with his heart. Mr Malik looked up from his Nescafé and gave a small smile.

'No, my dear, nothing.'

If it wasn't anything to do with his heart perhaps it was that accident he had told her about. Fancy trying to drive on a flat tyre – no wonder he had rolled the car and smashed the window and dented the roof. What on earth was he doing going all that way to that silly village with Benjamin? Yes, exactly what *had* he been doing? There was something funny going on.

She must remember to ask Benjamin.

Chicken

40

The temperature in the kitchen of the Suffolk Hotel is a hundred and rising. All ovens are aglow, all hotplates afire. Curries simmer, birianis boil – devilled shrimps, lamb chops and chicken wings sizzle and bake. Through the back door the aroma of roasting meat wafts in on the breeze. Just outside, on three large spits over charcoal fires, are three whole sheep. They have been cooking since noon. In the prep room three hundred curry puffs and an equal number of cocktail samosas (meat and vegetarian) are lined up on their metal trays ready for a final blasting in the oven. Six hundred vol-au-vent cases await their fillings. The head chef himself is adding the final fancy icing to the cakes. An hour to go before the ball.

In the breakfast room, which has been set up for drinks service, eight full cases of Johnnie Walker, eight of Hennessy and eight of Gordon's stand at the ready behind the bar. In the cold room is enough Tusker beer, tonic water and soda water to float a small herd of hippos. From the flower- and foliage-bedecked ballroom comes a screech as Milton Kapriadis tests the microphone. He has already set up music stands and drum kit and is now fiddling with wires and amplifiers. Past experience has taught him that it is best not to leave these things to others. From an old blue valise he removes some sheaves of music and begins to distribute them around the music stands. Top of the pile is the 'Blue Danube Waltz' – the old Glenn Miller arrangement. It has been first dance at the Hunt Club Ball since long before he started playing there. Next will be a foxtrot, then a two-step, a quickstep and on to a nice fast rock and roll medley. After the first break another waltz. Later in the evening he might get the band to play a couple of disco numbers – well, one has to keep up with the times. At Number 12 Garden Lane, Mr Malik is sitting in his pyjamas in front of the television.

Now the guests have arrived. Milton Kapriadis raises his baton. His Excellency the British High Commissioner to Kenya takes his wife by the hand and steps on to the floor for the first dance. Harry Khan turns to the woman beside him at the table.

'How about it, baby? Shall we dance or shall we dance?'

With a gracious smile, she assents. Arm in arm they take to the floor. Other couples join them. Hands clasped, his arm around her, they one-two-three, one-two-three around the floor behind the High Commissioner and his wife. Harry winks. Suddenly he and his partner spring apart. Still facing each other, they crouch then step to the right, step to the left. They twirl – what has happened to the waltz? Taking opposite hands he guides her under his raised arm, stops, and passes back. More twirls, more steps – and isn't that a sugar push? Rock and roll dancing in 3/3 time? In all the seventy years of the Hunt Club Ball no one has seen anything like it.

Not everyone is dancing. At a table for four near the buffet sit Jonathan Evans and his wife and Patsy King and her husband. Jonathan will ask Patsy for the next dance and she will coldly decline – thus ensuring, they hope, that their spouses will continue to suspect nothing of their illicit love. Other Old Hands from the Tuesday bird walks are sitting, glasses full before them, at a table nearby. Hilary Fotherington-Thomas (gin and tonic) and Joan Baker (brandy and soda) sit side by side inspecting the dance floor. Both longstanding members of the Karen Club, they form two-fifths of the Hunt Club Ball Committee. Two seats at their table are still vacant – Tom Turnbull has no doubt been having trouble with his bow tie or his Morris Minor, perhaps both (being on the committee, Hilary and Joan know just who has bought tickets). Nor yet any sign of Rose.

For the woman Harry is dancing with is not Rose Mbikwa. He had phoned from the Asadi Club and left a message, and she had later phoned him at his hotel. She was, she said, extremely flattered that he should ask her but she had already made other arrangements. Harry has instead persuaded his mother to come. She has never been to a Hunt Club Ball and is, despite her grumbling that the music is too loud and there is too little curry in the curry puffs, having a fine old time. Also in the party are Harry's pretty niece Elvira, with her brother Sanjay and his girlfriend. Finally there is Elvira's fiancé, just back from Dubai and at this moment looking none too happy – perhaps because the woman Harry is now dancing with is Elvira. For the last two nights they have been practising moves (not all of them, I have to say, strictly vertical) in his hotel bedroom and right now she seems to be having a hoot.

But Harry Khan and Sanjay Bashu are not the only members of the Asadi Club to have bought tickets to the Hunt Club Ball. At a table on the other side of the room Mr and Mrs Patel are seated between Mr and Mrs Gopez and the Singhs. The Tiger is tuxedoed, Mrs Singh is looking radiant in pink. Mr Patel is wearing the special smile that can only come from winning a recent bet with Mr Gopez. Two seats at their table are also unoccupied.

'Think he'll come?' said Mr Gopez.

'I don't know, A.B.,' said Mr Patel. 'I really don't know.'

'Well, Daddy, how do I look?'

Mr Malik, still in his pyjamas, looked up from BBC World

News. And what did he see? His daughter Petula, and not wearing jeans. He smiled, then his brow furrowed. That sari of deep crimson trimmed with narrow gold – was it not one her mother used to wear? And that little sparkling bindi on her forehead, was that not just like the one her mother would have worn? True, his daughter's hair was not the long dark tresses that his wife would wrap behind her head to show her slender neck to such melting effect, but Petula's short hair was shining like ebony, and yes, those were surely her mother's gold and ruby earrings dangling from her dear small ear lobes.

'My daughter,' he said, and tears came into his eyes. 'You look beautiful. Where are you going?'

'To the ball, of course.'

'The ball?'

'The Hunt Club Ball. Hurry up, we'll be late.'

'Late – us?'

'Daddy, I saw the tickets. I got the hint. Come on.'

'I . . .'

'Come on, Daddy. A girl can't go to the ball all by herself, you know.'

She smiled at him and because more tears came into his eyes, he had to look away.

Mr Malik went into his bedroom and opened the camphor-wood wardrobe. He took down dinner jacket, trousers and shirt. He shaved and showered. The trousers and the jacket were a little tight, but the trousers had an adjustable waistband and he could leave the jacket unbuttoned. At least his black lace-up shoes still fitted. He went to the dressing table and tied his bow tie, then picked up the comb and, bending further towards the mirror, carefully arranged his hair.

'Well, daughter,' said Mr Malik as he re-entered the sitting room, 'how do I look?'

'Daddy,' she said. 'You look beautiful.'

★   ★   ★

Benjamin had been surprised when Petula had asked him what had happened that day out at his village but was only too happy to tell her about the birds and the bandits. And then he told her the rest of the story, as told to him by the barman at the Asadi Club while he was drinking his Coca-Cola (not being a member, he felt under no obligation not to divulge this privileged information). So Petula had found out all about her father's wager with Harry Khan and the tickets to the ball. She had figured the rest out herself. And she had known what she must do.

She insisted they drive her little Suzuki to the Suffolk Hotel, not her father's car.

'It will be much easier to park.'

And she was right because she managed to squeeze it into a spot just over the road from the hotel where the old green Mercedes would never have fitted. Taking his beautiful daughter on his arm, Mr Malik walked her across the road and up the steps into the lobby. From the ballroom to the left they could hear a blast from the horn section. The first set was over. A waiter hurried from the kitchen, two trays of mushroom vol-au-vents held high on spread fingers. They followed him into the ballroom through the open double doors.

Mr Patel was the first to spot them. He stood.

'Over here, Malik.'

The dancers were returning to their seats and it took a little while for Mr Malik and Petula to reach the table and greet his friends.

'Glad you made it, old boy,' said Mr Gopez. 'Beginning to think you wouldn't.'

'How could I not?' said Mr Malik, glancing towards his daughter and finding tears once more in his eyes. So, so like her mother tonight.

'Everybody seems to be here,' said Mr Gopez. 'I suppose you spotted Harry Khan. He's been dancing – with that niece of his, you know.'

Mr Malik looked around the room. Yes, there was Harry Khan

now sitting at a table with the girl and Sanjay Bashu and two others who Mr Malik supposed were his mother and some other member of the family. At another table he could see some of his friends and acquaintances from the Tuesday bird walk. He couldn't spot Rose Mbikwa but saw Joan Baker rise from the table and go over to the microphone. The room became quieter.

'Your Excellency, ladies and gentlemen. Supper is served at the buffet.'

In the moment's silence that followed her announcement those nearest the windows could hear the slam of a car door, followed by a curse and a click, then another slam. A minute later Tom Turnbull entered the ballroom. His dinner jacket was at least as old as his car. On his arm, sheathed in a dark blue satin dress and pale blue shawl, was Rose Mbikwa.

Neither Mr Malik nor Harry Khan had considered that Rose might have another admirer. That every year for the last ten years, she might have received the same invitation. It was never made personally at the Tuesday morning bird walk, it always came by post – Mr Tom Turnbull requests the pleasure of the company of Mrs Rose Mbikwa to the Nairobi Hunt Club Ball. Each year she had penned a kind refusal. The subject would not be mentioned again until the next invitation arrived. This year for some reason, Rose had said yes. Even Rose herself was not sure why she had done so. Perhaps it was something to do with her operation and seeing things better now, differently. Perhaps it was something to do with Harry Khan and having fun. Perhaps it was even something to do with Mr Malik.

Rose had, thought Mr Malik, never looked so lovely. She let go of Tom Turnbull's arm and greeted Joan and Hilary with light hugs. Mr Malik saw her catch Harry Khan's eye and smile and wave. People from other tables began drifting towards the buffet. Rose looked around the room, apparently searching for someone else. When she looked in his direction and smiled Mr Malik could not help turning round to see who was behind him.

Rose bent towards the other women now seated at the table and murmured a few words, then made her way through the crowd towards him, still smiling.

'Mr Malik,' she said, 'I hoped I would find you here.'

'Mrs Mbikwa. I think I hoped the same.'

'You must excuse me,' said Rose. 'Mr Malik, I promise not to keep you from your friends – or your supper – for long, but do you have a moment?'

She led him past the buffet, back through the double doors into the lobby and over to the reception desk.

'Could I have the package I left here just now please?'

The desk clerk handed over a plastic bag. She reached inside and pulled out something blue, singed and soggy.

'Hilary told me you had bought tickets so I thought I should take the opportunity tonight of delivering this in person. It *is* yours, isn't it, Mr Malik?'

Mr Malik looked down at what was left of his missing notebook.

'It is indeed mine, Mrs Mbikwa. But how did you . . .'

'I found it just outside my house. In Serengeti Gardens, you know. It was on a bonfire, not far from where your car was left the other day. I noticed the bird on the front and I thought I recognized it. I suppose it must have fallen out of the car or been thrown out. I'm sorry, it seems to have got slightly burned, and rather wet too. It was raining.' She put the book into his hand. 'It doesn't have your name on it but I was sure it must be yours. I thought you might want it back. All those notes.'

'Yes, I . . .'

'Good. Well, why don't we just leave it safe here at the desk and you can pick it up when you go.'

'Yes, I shall indeed do that. Thank you. May I say, Mrs Mbikwa, that I am very relieved to get it back. More than you might know.'

Rose smiled and looked into his eyes.

'Yes, I thought you would be.'

At that moment Milton Kapriadis raised his baton for the next dance to begin.

'Oh, the Vienna waltz,' said Rose as she heard the first notes. 'It used to be one of my husband's favourites.' She leaned towards him and put a soft hand on his forearm. 'Mr Malik – or should I say Mr Dadukwa? Would you, I wonder, care to dance?'

And so, to the music of Milton Kapriadis and his Safari Swingers, we must leave the Nairobi Hunt Club Ball. On the dance floor of the Suffolk Hotel Mr Malik is holding in his arms the woman of his dreams, who is smiling at him with a most tender smile. If at this moment he is not the happiest short, round, balding brown man in all the world then I don't know what happiness is. We see his eyes turn towards his daughter Petula, who is also on the floor. In gold-trimmed crimson sari she looks as lovely as ever her mother did – and is that Harry Khan's niece's fiancé she is dancing with? He is gazing into her eyes, she into his, and they seem to be very happy too. Harry Khan has taken his niece Elvira to sit with his fellow members of the Asadi Club, and he must have told them some joke for they are all laughing. Perhaps it is a story about Bill Clinton, or about one of the American franchisees' wives. I hope he isn't saying anything about how Mr Malik got that old school nickname, because I never shall.